DELIVERANCE

NYC DOMS BOOK 1

JANE HENRY

I dedicate Deliverance to every reader whose life has been touched in some way by a child with special needs. You are as special as they are. This story is for you.

ACKNOWLEDGMENTS

A big thank you to Shannon from Shanoff Designs for an *amazing* cover, to my editor and proofers who helped me in more ways I can say, and for the enthusiasm and support of my review team and Club members. Thank you!

CHAPTER 1

"You son of a bitch," I hiss, intentionally keeping my voice low. Crazy, half-cocked, vindictive ex-lover isn't normally my thing.

Hell, there's a first for everything, though.

"Diana! *Stop.* This is stupid, and girl, you *know* I know stupid when I see it because I've done *all the stupid* in my life." Beatrice pleads with me to think twice as she shuffles toward me, trying to place her small frame between me and the car I'm about to destroy.

"Stop the lecture." My hands tremble as I hold the keys, glaring past my blonde-haired, blue-eyed bestie, and focusing my hatred on the silver Maserati. I march past Beatrice, and before I can change my mind, dig the tip of my key into the gleaming exterior with maniacal glee. Crouching down, I take grim pleasure in destroying the most beautiful car I've ever looked at. Sat in. Been fucked in.

"Did you tell Little Miss High and Tight your sob story?" I cackle to the car as if it's my ex-boyfriend embodied. I'd only just met the guy a few weeks ago, my first real boyfriend since my ex-husband took off, but I'd managed to convince myself he was *the one.* My savior. My hero. With a particularly vicious swipe, I lose my footing and nearly sprawl onto the snowy sidewalk, but I catch myself on the bumper. Wind whips at my hair, icy snow lashing my bare skin, but I hardly feel it.

Tequila for the win.

"Diana," Beatrice cajoles. "You've had too much to drink. God, woman! Get ahold of yourself! You've done it, okay? You've done enough. I shouldn't have let you out of the car. This isn't *you.* You're too smart to pull this teenaged shit. Just get in the car and I'll—"

"Leave me alone." I love this girl to death, but I don't trust myself not to shove her out of my way if she tries to stop me. I scrape the key once more, so deep it feels like fucking nails on a chalkboard, but I like knowing the damage will be severe. "You don't know what it's like to walk into your bedroom and see some bitch with her lips wrapped around your boyfriend's cock."

Scrraaape.

"You don't know what it's like to see betrayal in the eyes of the man who said he loved you."

Scraaaape.

"You don't know what it's like," my voice catches on a dry sob, so I underscore my angst with another cut of the key, "to have to explain to your son that the bastard who promised to take him to the drive-in movie theater was a lying piece of shit who'll never come back."

Scrape, scrape, scraaape.

Sitting back on my heels, I eye the destruction with triumph.

Beatrice talks to me like one might speak to a rabid animal, her hands outstretched in a gesture meant to calm. "I may not know those things, but I do know that—" She freezes, her voice now panicked. "Oh. Oh, *shit.* Diana, stop. Oh my *God.* We have to go."

But before I can respond, the deep growl of a man's voice right behind me—a voice *I do not know*—makes me nearly stumble.

"What the *fuck* are you doing to my car?"

Shit.

His... car?

I turn, my cheeks hot despite the freezing cold, to stare into the terrifyingly furious face of the biggest man I've ever seen. He towers over me, even wearing my tallest spiky heels, and the involuntary step I take back helps me see him better. Everything about him is dark, with his swarthy skin and nearly-black hair, but it's his eyes—black as coal beneath thick, heavy brows, that pin me in place. I can't move. I can't speak. I can barely think.

His jaw, covered in thick, dark stubble, tightens when his huge, muscled arms cross his expansive chest.

In any other time or place, I'd find the man sexy as fuck. But now?

"Your car?" I whisper.

"My car," he says in a low growl. "What are you doing to *my* fucking car?"

I blow out a breath and close my eyes.

I'm screwed.

CHAPTER 2

I BREATHE in deeply through my nose and exhale through my mouth, my chest rising and falling with the effort of staying calm. I'd learned to master my temper at an early age, and it rarely flares like it does tonight. Something about catching some crazy bitch with wild hair, a short skirt, and spiky red heels keying your car does that to a guy.

I narrow my gaze on her, trying to figure out who the fuck she is. Someone I know? A scorned ex? Nah. A submissive I'd topped at my club? No. There's nothing familiar about her at all.

I'd have remembered this one.

A mane of wild, unruly black curls that frame her oval-shaped face. Large hazel eyes with ridiculously long lashes. A small, pert nose, full mouth with cherry-red lips. She doesn't come anywhere near my height, but wearing those death-defying heels, she's taller than any woman I've known. Though she meets my gaze squarely, she can't hide the tremble in her lower lip, betraying her fear.

"*Your* car?" she asks.

The little blonde standing next to her gives an audible

gasp that ends with a squeak, and covers her mouth with her hand, then spins around to look at my plate covered in a layer of ice and snow.

"*My* car. That's parked outside of *my* club." I jerk a thumb at my chest, then to the plain brick building with the shiny black door, the entrance to Verge, the exclusive BDSM club. My second home.

She whips her head around and gazes at the door, then looks back to me. Her eyes narrow and her lips tighten. "You're lying."

Oh, the little shit. The fucking *gall* of her to defile my car, then sass me like that. What I wouldn't give to take her across my knee and teach her some manners.

With another intake of breath to keep me calm, I whip out my cell. "Let me call my friend, Zack. Local NYPD. I'm sure he'll be happy to haul your ass to jail and press charges for me."

Real fear crosses her features then. "No! Oh, God." She turns back to the car, wavering on her feet, and scrapes ice and snow off the plate.

Is it the heels, or is she *drunk?* Christ, if that girl were mine she'd pay for this.

"Wrong plate," she moans. "Oh, *God.* It's a New York plate. This *is* the wrong car." She shivers, then. Is she cold, afraid, or both?

"No shit," I snap. "We're in fucking *New York City.* What'd you expect?"

She spins around and waves her hands in front of her, pleading for leniency.

"I am *so* sorry. Whatever the damage is, I'll pay for it, I swear to God, every last penny. I didn't mean..." she turns to the car and brings a hand to her mouth, eyes filling with tears.

"I... this is..." she shakes her head and pulls out her wallet, taking out a shiny gold credit card. "This isn't me. This isn't what I do."

What forced her hand?

Fuck me. I want to know.

"I'll—I'll pay for the damage." The wind picks up. She wraps her arms around herself, dressed in a thin leather jacket, her hands beet red from the cold.

Seeing her freezing cold, eyes brimming with unshed tears, I make a decision.

She'll pay for it alright. I'll drag her ass out of the cold, though, and we'll take it from there.

"My office is just inside that building. Come and we'll talk about this."

Her frantic gaze sweeps from her friend to me. The blonde shakes her head, and they have a hissed conversation before the woman pushes her friend's hand off her shoulder and turns to me. "I'll go. I promise, I'll make it up to you."

That she will.

I don't trust her not to run away, so when she gets in the car idling by the curb, and she makes her way to the door, I grip her arm. "Ice, heels, and whatever the fuck you've got coursing through your veins, I don't need a liability on my hands." Part of me wonders what the fuck I'm doing, taking the girl into Verge. Pretending the feel of her small arm in my hand doesn't make me want to touch more of her.

Non-members don't grace the halls of Verge, and though I've been with many a submissive inside the club, I've never taken someone in. It's crossing a line somehow.

But this woman is not mine, I tell myself. Not a date. I'm bringing her in from the cold and exchanging information. Making sure she doesn't take off and screw me over.

She'll catch frostbite out there.

Yeah.

She doesn't have to see anything. Nothing suspicious. Keep her in the office, then get her the fuck out of here.

Right.

I nod to Brax, the bouncer at the door tonight, who eyes the woman next to me with curiosity. I shake my head, once. *No, she isn't mine.*

If she were mine, she wouldn't be sitting pretty for long.

Stalking down the hall I release her and order, "Keep your eyes on me. No snooping. This is a members-only, private club, and you're not welcome here."

She huffs out a mirthless laugh. "Seriously? Like I asked to come here? Listen, mister, I'll give you my information and get the hell out of here."

"You'll take a seat in my office and sober your ass up first." I open the door to my office and grab the chair in front of my desk, the sound of the feet scraping along the varnished floor jarring.

"No thanks, I'll stand."

"Sit."

"No."

I spin around to look at her. Her eyes flash with warning, her jaw clenched in anger.

"We can do this the easy way…" my voice is controlled, a low purr that makes submissives under my authority quiver. But not this woman. "…or the hard way."

"Oh yeah?" she asks through clenched teeth, stepping over to me, her hazel eyes meeting mine. "Some chicks might dig this whole *caveman* shit, but I don't. There is no *easy* or *hard* way. There is *one* way. You give me a piece of paper and a pen, and I give you my insurance information. We contact them in the morning and file a report. They handle the rest, and we never see each other," she flicks her wrist for emphasis, *"again."*

I shake my head with a chuckle, ignoring how her sass makes my dick hard. Jesus, I haven't had a woman defy me like this in far too long. "You committed an act of vandalism, sweetheart." I let the words drip sarcasm, needing her to feel this. "Your insurance company won't fucking compensate for intentional damage. I either press charges, or we handle this off the books."

She bristles at the "sweetheart," but her bravado slips. Her eyes betray her fear. "Oh," she says in a little voice.

I shake my head. I never dreamed she'd give me shit like this. It'd been a mistake not to call the police.

"On second thought, maybe Zack really does need to be involved." I take out my phone, but her eyes go wide and she grabs my arm.

"No! God, no, please don't. I have no idea what they'll do with my assistance if I get charged for this! And my son needs it. I can't risk that."

What?

"Please," she whispers.

Christ.

I stare at her and point to the chair once more. "Sit," I tell her, gentler this time. I lean back against my desk in front of her and watch as she sits.

Victory. A small one, but I'll take it.

"Your name?"

"Diana."

Diana. The name of a goddess. Fucking *Wonder Woman.*

"Tobias Creed," I say.

My phone buzzes, followed by a flash of light on my desk, a vibrant red that makes ice instantly pulse in my veins. A signal from Zack, one I can't ignore.

The flashing red has only been used once since Seth and I opened Verge: emergency lock-down.

Shit.

I push off the desk and point a finger at her. "You stay right there," I growl, taking my phone in hand. "I need to find out who triggered the alarm." She screws up her face to protest, but the imminent danger makes me angry.

"Your ass leaves that chair, and your ass is *mine.* I don't care who the hell you are, you leave now and you won't sit for a fucking week." Her eyes widen, and I frown at her, pinning her in place with my gaze. I am beyond caring about etiquette, my dose of mercy used up. "Try me, Diana."

She opens her mouth in outrage and pushes her hands on the arm rests, but I just repeat, *"Try me."*

She sits back down with a huff.

Good.

I'll sort her ass out later.

I turn the door to my office as I answer the call. "Yeah?"

"Creed." I recognize Zack's gritty voice. "Club's in lockdown. No one leaves. On my way in now. I told Seth to start the lockdown."

What the fuck is this about?

"Victim of sexual assault, and all signs point to the perpetrator originating from Verge. Victim's friend says she was there tonight, left with a stranger. You do not reveal details to your team yet. No one, and I mean *no one,* leaves your place without express permission from me or another officer."

Acid burns in my stomach, my hands clench into fists. With a growl, I hit the master lock by the door and can almost hear the audible *click* as the four exits to Verge shut tight.

"How bad?" I ask, bracing myself. Running a club in downtown NYC means I'm no stranger to crime, but when it involves sexual assault—

Zack pauses, and when he speaks his voice is tight. "Vicious. Cruel. She was found on the corner of Trace and Main, was rushed to County. Intensive care."

Fuck.

My blood turns cold as sirens ring through the night.

CHAPTER 3

THE BITTER OUTRAGE I felt at the Neanderthal's high-handed commands evaporates at the sound of sirens. I know, even though I can't hear the conversation on the other end of the line, that something terrible happened. I can tell by the way Tobias's jaw tightens, and his body straightens.

Chad.

Oh, God. If anything happened to my son...

Reaching for my phone, I text the sitter. No response.

He's fine. I tell myself while breathing deep, willing my nerves to calm. *He's going to be fine.* I focus on counting backward from ten, my chest constricting, but it doesn't help. The room feels too warm, my head too light. I blink. The lights brighten then darken then brighten again. I don't notice I'm on my feet and holding my breath until I feel warm, strong hands on me. I gasp for breath.

"Sit," he orders, and this time it isn't the harsh command of a few moments ago, but softer. "What the fuck's goin' on here? You okay?"

I shake my head and close my eyes, trying to breathe through my nose. "Anxiety attack," I gasp out, panting now.

"I... get them sometimes." A band tightens on my chest. My head is light and woozy, the room spins. My lungs are too empty, and that's not okay, I need to breathe air into them but whatever pushes against my chest won't let me. Panic wells up and I gasp.

"Christ, lay down on the couch." He leads me over to a couch pushed up against a wall, and he pushes me onto it, kneeling his large frame in front of me. "Hold my hand," he orders. I need this. No questions. Just listen.

I do what he says. His hand is large and warm and rough, and it shocks me how quickly the band in my chest loosens.

"Breathe in through your nose," he says. Eyes still closed, I obey. "There. Now breathe steadily. If you can handle it, sit up, but do not move. I have things to do."

I nod. It's embarrassing, losing my shit like this. I haven't had an anxiety attack in over a year.

Fucking tequila.

I lift my phone, breathing in relief when a text message flashes on my screen

It's Mandy, my son's babysitter. *I'm sorry, Mrs. McAdams. Everything's fine here. Chad's asleep, and I had headphones on, studying, and didn't see your message.*

Tears prick the back of my eyes.

This is why I don't go out.

This is why I only hire babysitters when my friends practically drag me, kicking and screaming.

No one takes care of Chad the way I do. No one gets him. The big, bossy bear of a man stands in the doorway to his office, his head tilting toward me to keep an eye on me, but I sit up quickly when I see uniformed officers in the hall. My stomach clenches, but I breathe deep and focus on staying calm.

A tall, burly man dressed in plain clothes, but obviously a detective or some kind of police officer, approaches Tobias.

He has light brown hair and deep brown eyes. He speaks in a husky, controlled voice. "We need to question every dungeon monitor and member of your staff," he says. "Seth gave the signal. You've locked the facility down?"

Tobias nods and my heart kicks up a beat.

Dungeon monitor? Lockdown?

Tobias' gaze pivots around to lock eyes with mine, probably afraid I'm going to lose my shit again. I stare him back, daring him to accuse me of being a wimp. Swinging my legs over the side of the couch, I'm about to approach them when I remember what brought me here. There is a police officer standing in front of him. One sentence is all it would take for him to report me. What would happen then? If I get in trouble with the law… if Chad loses his funding… too much is at stake.

My eyes meet his, and I silently plead.

He doesn't look away when he speaks to the police officer. "Zack, I have company here tonight. Sorry, should've told you."

Zack just comes in and extends his hand. "Nice to meet you…?" His voice trails off, inviting me to give him my name.

"Diana McAdams," I say, my mouth dry. "Nice to meet you, too."

Tobias addresses Zack. "Brax is on at the door, Travis tending bar. I'll have to look to see who's on the floor."

Zack pulls a notebook out of his back pocket and starts writing things down.

"You haven't seen Axle?"

"No, but I—oh for Christ's sake, Zack. Axle doesn't like to kill spiders, never mind hurt a—" his gaze swings around to me again, and he stops. "It couldn't be him."

Zack frowns. "It's never who you think it is."

Tobias swears, but several police officers rush past them and he quiets, then turns to me. "I need to see to a few things.

Stay here, and for God's sake, don't—" He looks around. "Christ, I can't leave her here." He turns back to Zack. "Not until we know for sure it's safe."

What the hell?

"I wouldn't," Zack says. "Good call."

Tobias purses his lips and frowns. "Diana, come with me." He extends his hand to me. I stare, not sure how to respond. "Just… try not to look around too much. Don't judge, just focus on me."

Um. What?

"Tobias, I need to go home."

Something inside me says he isn't gonna let me go, but I have to try. "My son needs me. If he wakes up and I'm not there, he'll freak."

Zack shakes his head. "No one goes anywhere until we've lifted the lockdown for everyone. I'm sorry, but you have to stay." I open my mouth to protest, but he shakes his head again. "You'll have to follow instructions, ma'am."

Ma'am? I am only thirty-one years old, *thankyouverymuch.*

I blink at him as if he spoke a foreign language. "What?"

"You can't go," he repeats. "Not until we've interrogated everyone here tonight and gotten word it's safe to release them."

I don't even know where I am, I want to say. But I have to play it safe and not draw attention to why I'm here.

Tobias looks at me before he talks. "Need to talk to her alone. Give us five?"

Zack nods. "Make it quick." He joins the officers in the hallway, and Tobias shuts the door.

"Who's your son with?" he asks in a controlled but gentle voice, as if he's afraid I'll lose my shit again.

"A babysitter," I say, shaking my head. He won't understand. How can he?

"How old's your son?" he asks, his arms crossed on his

chest, staring at me with those dark, probing eyes that make me feel naked and exposed.

I swallow. "Eight."

He frowns slightly. "Eight? And he won't understand if he wakes up and you're not there?"

God.

I close my eyes and inhale briefly, willing myself to ignore the anxiety that threatens to choke me. I open my eyes. "He… doesn't handle surprises well. He needs structure and routine and predictability."

His brows furrow. I exhale, and continue. "He's on the spectrum," I say, willing my voice to stay steady. "Though he's—he's high functioning."

Tobias's eyes soften, and he nods, slowly. Damn, I can't take his sympathy. It'll make me cry, and I don't want that. The small gesture of compassion loosens the knot in my chest, and tears blur my vision. *Fuck.* I blink them back and take another deep breath, my voice dropping to a whisper. "But I have to get home. Listen, I'm so sorry about your car. I swear to God I'm good for the damage. This isn't *me.* This isn't what I do. I don't know what came over me. I'll give you every means to contact me you need."

Tobias shakes his head, uncrosses his arms, and steps closer to me. "I'm sorry, Diana. Listen, I hear you, but I can't let you go home right now."

"Please," I beg.

He shakes his head with finality. "I can't. Our entire facility is on lockdown."

Dread gnaws my stomach. "Where *are* we? What is this place?"

Tobias smiles grimly. "Welcome to Verge. New York City's most reputable BDSM club."

A nervous giggle bubbles up. "I—you—can't be serious," I say, shaking my head, welcoming the comic relief. "You're *joking.* BDSM? Like *Fifty Shades of Grey* BDSM?" He shrugs a shoulder. "And that's legal here?"

His deep chuckle sends shivers down my spine. "Of course it's legal. That officer I'm friends with? He's a member here and believe me, that guy's as law-abiding as they come."

My jaw drops. "Are you *kidding* me?"

He rolls his eyes. "For God's sake, it isn't what you think it is."

But before we can talk further, a knock comes at the door.

"I didn't want to have to bring you in there, yet, but you'll have to come with me now." He leans in, his large, strong body brushing up against mine, and fixes me with a stern look. "Stay by my side and do what I say." His voice lowers, his brows furrowing. "Do that and you'll be fine."

I huff out a laugh. Suddenly, the whole thing seems preposterous. I'm with a… master or whatever? At a BDSM Club? For real? "Whatever you say… *sir.*" I snicker, but he only opens the door, his jaw tight.

"Watch it, Diana."

I walk by his side, surprised that my body responds instinctively. His deep voice resonates through my limbs, his commanding nature sending a reluctant throb to my lady parts.

Shit.

I smirk to myself as I walk out of his office. One thing's for sure. Beatrice will think this is *epic.*

CHAPTER 4

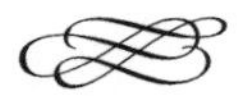

I REACH for her hand as we leave the office. Her eyes widen as if startled, and she takes in a ragged breath, but doesn't take my hand. Her hand shook when I held it in the office, but now she pulls away from me, and tucks her arms across her chest. We walk so closely, though, I could touch her if I wanted to. And God, I want to.

She's gorgeous. My stomach warms at the feel of her skin brushing mine as we round the corner and enter the hallway. It isn't just her curvy, vivacious body or fetching eyes. Or the full lips I want to take between my teeth. Or the round, beautiful ass that needs a good, hard session. It's the ardor that stokes who she is. The woman is fire and ice.

My office sits at the entrance to Verge, and beyond that, a long hallway leads to the lobby where guests discuss limits. Contracts are offered. Couples meet here before entering the more populated rooms. The first doorway opens to the heart of Verge, a bar and dance floor, and another leads to the dungeon, the party room, and private rooms.

As we near the lobby, Diana's body tightens, and her breathing becomes louder, labored.

"Breathe, Diana," I remind her. She gives me a quick nod, and her chest rises with the exertion as she lets out a breath slowly.

"Got it," she says. "I'm fine, really." She hugs her arms tighter across her chest.

Zack approaches, pushing his way between us. "Everyone on staff is accounted for," he says. "Of course, I can't speak for all the dominants who come here, though. We'll have to do the best we can with what we've got."

"I've got the name of every dominant who's ever crossed this threshold," I say. Zack merely nods as he walks through the lobby to the bar, Diana following. The relaxed atmosphere of the bar changes when he walks in with me. Voices hush, and couples that were slouched together on the couch sit upright, all eyes on the three of us.

The entryway opens to a large area, with a bar against one wall. The lighting is dim, soft jazz streams through speakers. We try to keep Verge classy. Though the crowds are heavier on Friday evenings, the main dance floor is often the least populated area in the club. Behind the bar to the left are doorways that lead to the... *kinkier* areas of Verge.

I'll keep her in the main room. Whatever trust I've established in the brief interactions we've had thus far could vanish completely if she looks into the rooms beyond the bar. I know if she catches a glimpse of someone roped to the St. Andrew's Cross, she'll lose her mind.

"Not much play in the bar area," I say to her as all eyes follow us. "But beyond the bar are the dungeon, party, and private rooms. All consensual. All safe. All sane."

Zack whips his head around and shoots me a probing look, but I dismiss him with a quick shake of my head.

"Master Tobias." The low drawl arrests my attention, though I don't even need to look to know who's talking. The only Verge member who speaks with a drawl is Travis, a ruggedly handsome bartender, and youngest member of our staff.

I give him a chin lift. "Travis."

"What's goin' on?" He wipes his hand on a bar towel and tucks the towel into the waistband of his thick leather belt, then brushes his longish sandy-brown hair out of his eyes. "I hear there's a lockdown?"

"Shh," I warn. "We'll keep it as brief as we can. One at a time, we need reports from each member of the staff."

Travis raises a brow. "Oh?"

I lean into the bar and speak in a low voice. "Sexual assault this evening, victim may have ties to the club. Everyone has to be questioned."

He whistles, his brows drawing together and his jaw clenching. "Son of a bitch," he mumbles. "Someone we know?"

"Not someone I recognize. Friend says she hasn't been here in a while but returned tonight. I need you to go back to my office with Zack. I'll man the bar." I take my place behind the bar as Travis leaves with Zack.

Diana looks around with wide eyes. "Doesn't *look* like a BDSM club," she mumbles. "Looks… normal."

I snort. "And what exactly do *you* think a BDSM club looks like? Cuz Lord knows you haven't set foot in one."

She crosses her arms on her chest. "Oh yeah? How'd you know I've never been in one? I could be, like—a BDSM club expert or designer."

My shoulders shake with laughter. "*Designer?* Like, let me interest you in these handmade spanking benches, sir? The pine with velvet-wrapped cuffs enhance the décor."

She smiles, her lips quirking up at the edges. It's the first time I've seen her smile all night. Her face lights up like daisies blooming. "I'd recommend something sturdier than *pine* for a spanking bench," she says, "assuming there would be *impact.*"

"Oh?" I ask, as a customer approaches and orders a pint. I pull the beer from the tap, slide it onto the counter, and update his tab. "What might you recommend?"

"Cedar," she says, "or perhaps oak."

"I'm surprised. You don't strike me as the type who'd be familiar with the makings of a spanking bench." My cock thickens at the mere thought of her gorgeous body stretched over the bench, ass perched high, waiting for me to punish her. I grab a glass and fill it with water, snag a wedge of lemon, and slide it over to her.

She frowns. "I could use something a bit stronger than this if I'm sticking around all night."

I sober, leaning over the bar to speak into her ear above the noise around us. "Not on my watch. Did you forget how we met? You were sloshed and vandalizing my car. You can have water, seltzer, or ginger ale. You pick."

"How generous of you," she snaps, glaring.

"It is, thank you," I respond, choosing to ignore her snark.

A sharp slapping sound makes her jump. She cranes her neck behind her and gasps at the sight of a woman upended over a guy's lap.

"You let that happen in *public?*" She seems genuinely appalled.

"This is hardly public, Diana." I stifle a chuckle as the man places the woman back on the chair and she sits with her head lowered, chastened. "And, sweetheart, that's tame compared to what you'll find behind those doors." I gesture to the private rooms.

She gulps her drink as if wishing it was something stronger. She doesn't respond, but pulls out her phone and glances at it.

"All good at home?" I ask.

"Yeah," she says with a sigh of relief. "Thank God."

I fill drinks and watch her as she sips her water. "I could decorate a place like this," she muses after a while.

"Oh?"

"I'm an interior decorator. You *could* use a little help in the décor department, you know."

I grin at her. "People don't come here for the décor, babe."

She rolls her eyes and I stifle a growl, imagining what it would be like to fist that hair of hers and teach her to behave. I never allow my subs to roll their eyes at me.

She's not your sub.

"Such a male thing to say," she quips. "God, *they don't come here for the décor,"* she mocks. "Of course you'd say that. You've practically outfitted this place with moose antlers." She waves a hand around and shakes her head, not at all heeding my warning growl. "People don't *come* for the décor," she agrees with a nod. "But it affects the way they feel when they're here. Tell me this," she continues. "You go to a restaurant and order a sandwich, and it comes on paper plates with thin napkins, versus going to a place that has fine linens and tablecloths. Which do you feel is higher quality?"

"Depends. Best New York style pizza in the city is served on paper plates."

"Oh for God's sake."

"It's true. I go to a swanky place I expect to *pay* more, not necessarily get better quality."

She shakes her head. "Well, *you* are a man. How many of the people who come here are of the male variety?'

My lips twitch. "About half."

She nods. "Ask the females what they think," she says, and she shoots me a wink.

My cock pushes harder against my jeans. Christ, her snarky attitude entices me, begging to be fucked out of her.

"Master... Tobias?" I look up to find Philippa, a petite

brunette, standing near the bar. Something isn't right. She looks at me through tear-stained eyes, her cheeks red and puffy, then she looks to Diana.

"I don't mean to interrupt anything," she says in a husky whisper, her voice trembling.

I shake my head and place the bar mop down. "We were just chatting. You're not interrupting." She's one of my favorite clients. Ten years younger than I am, a natural submissive, she's too timid for my personal tastes but a sweet girl. I never pursue anything more than friendship with the women in my club. A journalist by day, Philippa keeps her nighttime club visits secret.

"I know the woman who was attacked," she whispers, her eyes filling with tears. "Do you?"

I shake my head. But now the reality of what we face really hits me. A woman within close proximity has been violently abused, a woman with connections to *my* establishment, and the women here… tonight… are at risk, the perpetrator still at large.

I reach out and gently touch her hand. "I'm so sorry. I didn't. Do you need to sit down and have a drink? They're investigating now. We'll do the best we can to get to the bottom of this."

She sits down and takes the glass I hand her, sips the water, and asks, "Something stronger, please?"

I smile. "Fireball?" Her dom teases her relentlessly for her penchant for the fiery whiskey.

She smiles weakly and nods.

I push the shot glass to her. "On the house, honey. Philippa, meet my friend Diana."

Philippa turns and offers her hand to Diana. I'm struck with the irony of calling Diana my friend after she's vandalized my car, but I don't want anyone getting the wrong impression. She sure as hell isn't *more* than a friend.

"It's all going to be okay," I reassure Philippa. "I promise, we'll protect our members as best we can. Okay?"

"Thank you, sir. Daddy's a bit late tonight, but he'll take good care of me when he gets here."

Diana sits up straighter. I ignore her apparent outrage. If she can't handle what's normal around here, it's her own damn fault. I don't make apologies for who I am. We welcome kinksters from all walks of life without judgment, and I live my own life without apology.

Diana looks at me with wide eyes. *"Daddy?"* she mouths.

I nod. She points a finger at me as if to ask, *you?*

I swallow a laugh, knowing neither woman would appreciate my amusement right now, and I shake my head. No, I'm not a Daddy, but I know plenty who are.

The women talk amicably as I wipe down the counter and serve drinks, and then I hear Diana say, "Yeah I'd love it if you'd show me around. A tour, maybe? Master Tobias hasn't had the chance."

Hell *no.*

"I don't think so," I start to say, but I'm interrupted by Zack returning.

"Boys caught a suspect. Your team is cleared for the time being, but tomorrow, you and I talk. Got it? Travis alerted your team on my instruction, so you can tell them all clear."

"Got it," I respond, grateful that the danger has apparently passed. I pull out my phone and start sending messages to my staff.

Lock down over. Open the doors. Notify me or Zack immediately with anything out of place and tell the others.

I scrub a hand across my eyes, then pinch my nose, inhaling deeply. I'm so fucking ready to go home. I groan inwardly when I remember my desecrated Maserati.

It's then I notice she's gone.

"No *fucking* way."

Travis returns to the bar, welcomes me with a chin lift, and pulls the next round of drinks, assuming his role at the bar once more.

I told her to stay put.

She wants a tour? I'll give her a fucking tour. The special edition, demonstrations provided free of charge.

CHAPTER 5

I WALK beside Philippa with my head down, feeling like a high-schooler sneaking to the back of the school for a forbidden smoke, knowing the potential for getting caught is high, riding the adrenaline rush. I only just met the stern man they call *Master,* but I already know he doesn't take too kindly to defiance. My conscience pricks me a bit.

You wrecked his car, and now you're pushing your luck.

But it's almost as if I can't help myself, like the pulse of music and crush of people in the room beyond the bar beckons me, promising me a dose of excitement in my lack-luster life filled with endless work and stress.

After all, hasn't the entire *night* been like a scene out of some weird movie?

"You've never been here before?" Philippa's soft voice is edged with a slight accent.

"Well, no."

Least said, soonest mended.

"Have you ever been to a BDSM club before?" The petite woman looks at me curiously, her brows elevated in surprise. Her chestnut-colored hair hits her chin as she swings her head to me, her dark brown eyes apprehensive. "Are you sure Master Tobias is okay with you being here without his permission?"

For Christ's sake, she has to be such a rule follower?

"Why would he bring me here if he didn't want me to see the place?" I respond. It surprises me how easily I'm able to mislead the girl. But I have to know. I have to see. I fear that tomorrow, I'll wake up and this will be all over, a mirage, the product of too much tequila and a full moon. Tomorrow, I'll mourn opportunity lost.

I need to see *now.*

"Well, okay." Philippa chews her lip and stands in the darkened hallway, crossing her arms over her chest, surveying the room beyond us. The sound of something striking something else catches my attention, and I swing my eyes to the scene just beyond the doorway. A large man wearing all black holds a long, flexible something in his hand. It's cylindrical and narrow, but at the very end is a little square of what looks like leather. He points to the bench. I can't hear what he's saying, but the woman he points to is rubbing her ass. She nods, turns, and leans over the bench.

My heartbeat races, my breath caught in my throat. Holy shit. He's going to spank her. Right here. In front of me, and everyone. I have to admire the woman. She's scantily clad and lusciously curvy, wearing fishnets and heels and some sort of short skirt and top that barely covers her. He stands beside her, places a hand on her lower back, brings the thing in his hand back, and snaps it across her ass. I stand, frozen in shock, not sure what surprises me most: that this takes place in front of a crowded room, or that for some reason I can't even begin to understand, I'm *turned on.* My panties dampen between my thighs, my clit throbs. I can hardly breathe.

The woman flinches but then arches her back, like she

wants him to spank her again. He smacks her ass again, and again, and again, each smack ratcheting my heartbeat up, blood pounding in my ears. I can't hear anything, I can barely see, my vision growing hazy with a rush of arousal and anticipation. I've never seen anything like this. I've never been into this. And yet, my whole body is on fire.

I become aware of the fact that Philippa is talking. "Master Braxton has been here since the founding of Verge. Master Tobias and Braxton are dependable, upright men, and other than my own dominant, I trust no one more than them." She smiles. "C'mon. This is where the kinky fun happens." Her dark eyes light up and her lips quirk up at the edges. "Remember to stay out of scenes and to do your best to reserve judgment." She pauses and tips her head to the side, her voice softening. "I remember my first night here as well. It was overwhelming, and some things that I saw were very much out of my comfort zone. Now, though, the people here are like family."

My heart slams against my rib cage, and my mouth feels like it's stuffed with cotton balls.

"Go on," I say in a husky whisper.

I follow her. Low voices and a hum of background music lend a sense of intimacy to the room despite the obvious presence of so many. My gaze follows the clink of metal. To the right, a man stands behind a woman, fastening her wrist to some sort of pole. She's covered from head to toe in black, her hair in pigtails, but I can't see her eyes because she wears a blindfold. Is it a whipping post or something? He lifts something in his hand, something black with folded strips of leather. Oh my *God.* With his foot, he nudges her feet apart so that her stance widens, her wrists above her head secured in the cuffs, but before I see what he does, I notice a woman in the corner leaning down and gently stroking her hand through the hair of a man who kneels at her feet. She looks younger than he is, but she's clearly the one who holds the power here, as he takes her hand and brings her fingers to his mouth in a kiss that's at once tender and hot.

To the left of them, a woman kneels on the floor beside a man who holds a stout chain that ends in a collar around the woman's neck. He tugs the collar, and she frowns at him, earning her a sharp pull of her hair. It's degrading and yet, somehow… the most erotic thing I've ever seen. My skin prickles with nerves, a flush of warmth and excitement heating me through.

Swallowing my gasp, I concentrate on following the nonplussed Philippa, who charges ahead like we're power walking at the local mall.

This isn't right, I tell myself, yet the image of the collared woman on her knees makes my breath catch.

It's the outrage, I tell myself. *You're horrified.*

But I'm… not. And the next sight makes my confused jumble of thoughts still. A small loveseat sits in the corner of the room, away from the circular tables where couples sit, mingling. A large man with tribal tattoos along his neck, snaking down and peeking out from the tight sleeves of his t-shirt, sits with a woman on his lap. His face bends down to hers, whispering in her ear, and the way he cradles her on his lap is so intimate and moving, a lump forms in my throat. The woman, dressed in black, slings her arms around the neck of the man who holds her. She whispers something in his ear, and his head falls back, his whole frame shaking with laughter before he tips her to the side and gives her ass a playful smack.

I want that.

The sudden, impulsive thought startles me.

"This is our main play area," Philippa says. She stands close to me but I can hardly hear her because of the hum of music, laughter, and chatter. "We have several lounge areas, tables for guests to mingle, demonstrations frequently, and lots of…" she pauses, as if looking for the right words, then smiles and continues, "equipment in our playground." I notice against one wall is an x-shaped wooden frame with straps attached at the top and bottom, as well as a table covered in velvet, and several padded benches. Close to the benches I see a string of hooks attached to the wall, and from the hooks hang various… weapons? What are they?

"Regulars like to use their own toys," she says. "But we have plenty here for exploration."

"Exploration," I repeat.

"Well, not everyone comes prepared," Philippa says with a small smile, then her face lights up. "Oh. He's here!"

My heartbeat spikes. Tobias? But no, a man who looks a good deal older than Philippa with a shaved head and thin goatee along the edge of a strong jaw comes to Philippa. She runs to him, practically leaping into his arms. He holds her close to his chest and kisses her forehead. Once more, my heart twists.

"They absolutely do not come prepared. In fact, I can say with certainty that *you* did not." The deep voice by my ear startles me so much I nearly scream as I whip my head around. I meet the fuming gaze of Tobias. His eyes are storm clouds, narrow and dark, his jaw so tight I swear I can hear the gnashing of his teeth. His arms are crossed on his chest, biceps bulging. My gaze drops to the floor, falling on his feet decked in pitch black boots, planted like solid trees.

Shit.

This was maybe not a super smart move.

"I would… likely agree with that," I say in a ragged breath. Wiping my clammy hands on my thighs, my heart pounds so hard I fear he'll hear it. What was I thinking? Why did I come here?

He leans in, his voice a dangerous purr as he speaks in my ear. "How was your tour, Diana? Like what you see here?"

"Oh, it's lovely," I chatter nervously, trying to sidestep him and head to the door. "Everyone is... lovely, just... *lovely,*" I stammer. I look helplessly at the door with the brilliant fluorescent "exit" sign to my right, and then back to the door we entered. "I think it's time I go. Thanks for your hospitality. But I'll just be..."

His low, dark chuckle arrests me, making my nipples furl and my panties dampen.

Shit.

"You think you'll disobey a direct instruction, after vandalizing my car, come in here despite my admonition not to, and I'll let you go with such a cursory tour?" He laughs, wrinkles forming around his eyes. "Hell no. You wanted a tour, honey? I'm going to give you a *tour.*"

I spin around to get away but he grabs me by the arm, not hard enough to hurt, but firm enough I can't get away. "You'll come with me now."

Ho-*ly shit.* No!

He half-drags me to a vacant padded bench, the furthest away from the crowd. "I'll be easy on you, though, babe."

Babe?

"You can leave your clothes on."

Fuck!

That's an option?

I want to protest. I want to tell him no and shove him away, keep my dignity and leave with my head held high, but somehow, I can't. Caught up in nervous excitement, in the presence of a pissed-off dominant. A dim part of my brain says *no, don't do this,* but my body has other thoughts.

"And this, my friend, is a spanking bench."

I shiver, trying to quell my nerves, but it's fruitless. He continues like a realtor. "This is where submissives assume the position. A nicely padded, comfortable place for discipline, especially of the long, drawn-out variety. Not as comfortable as, say, a dominant's *lap,* but a classic piece of furniture hand-crafted from solid wood." He speaks in a friendly salesman tone, as if he's showing me the in-ground pool of a swanky estate, or the vaulted ceiling of a mansion. Suddenly, his voice hardens and he barks out, "On the table."

I spin around to look at him but he shakes his head, one sharp *no,* and points to the padded bench.

It's got to be the tequila. I, Diana McAdams, am *not* the kind of girl who takes orders from a caveman. Yet, somehow, it's exactly what I do. The cool, padded bench beneath me presses up against my belly and breasts, my hands somehow knowing to grasp the little handles at the far end.

I squeal when his firm hands take my ankles and pry my legs apart, the soft clink of metal then a sharp tug reminding me of the restraints attached to the bench. Next, he does the same to my wrists. Once secured, I can't budge. It's then I begin to panic.

"Tobias. I don't need a... a... *tour* quite as... as thorough as this one."

His large, powerful body leans in close to me, and I'm momentarily dazzled by the scent of strength and masculinity, the brisk musk waking my senses and turning my sex into molten lava. The deep sound of his voice washes over me as he speaks in my ear. "Babe, this is *exactly* what you need."

So, clearly pissed-off Tobias exudes testosterone in waves.

I try to clench my legs together, but spread out and strapped down like this, I can't move. I'm afraid he'll realize my panties are soaked, like he'll smell the arousal on me. My clit throbs and my breasts tingle, and I need to somehow get away from this, it's too intense.

What. The. Fuck.

"And this," he continues, back to pleasant realtor tone, "is a wooden paddle, made of the finest varnished pine. This is a beginner's implement, thin and lightweight, capable of packing a solid sting without much lasting effect. I'm sure the acrylic or a leather-covered oak would be more appropriate for the tour *you* so desperately need, but I feel a beginner's demonstration would suit you best at this juncture."

God. *No!* A paddle? How will I be able to look at myself in the mirror tomorrow? "What? I—I think I'm fine," I stammer. "Really, Tobias, this is—this is not something I'm—I don't need."

"Oh you do."

"You can't!"

"Do you refuse consent?" he asks, the question taking me by surprise. What will he do if I do refuse? Call the cops?

I shake my head once, and that's all he needs.

The solid *whack* of the paddle on my upturned ass takes me more by surprise than anything. I utter an involuntary little squeak. But before I recover from the first smack, he brings the paddle down a second time, harder, the solid wood smacking against both of my cheeks at once.

"Ow!"

Without a word, as I pull against the restraints in stunned silence, he delivers four hard, firm smacks, pausing several seconds between strokes. No one around us even looks at us, but I feel as if they do, like there's a spotlight on my humiliating position. I squeeze my eyes shut and try to instinctively block my ass, forgetting that my wrists are bound.

"And that'll do for our tour," he says, replacing the paddle on the demonstration table beside us. The fire has gone out of his eyes, his voice softer now, no longer tight and angry. His anger is gone, but mine's just beginning.

"Let me outta these restraints, Tobias. I swear to God. I

can't believe you did that." I hiss, trying to avoid anyone noticing us. I need to hide my arousal with my indignation.

"Excuse me?" He walks to the head of the table and stands where I can see him. Crossing his arms on his broad chest, he eyes me with a stern, slightly amused smile. "You can't believe I did that? What exactly do you think you deserve for disobeying me and trespassing on my property?"

Disobeying him? Trespassing?

He shakes his head, eyes darkening as he stares at me. "I don't know where *you* come from, honey, but where I'm from, there are rules that govern behavior." He leans in, his low voice tight with authority. "We *met* because you vandalized my car. The only reason you were allowed past my office was because I brought you here. The rules of membership here state that only members and members' guests are allowed access to the dungeon. You were *not* brought here by me. Therefore, you trespassed."

My jaw drops, and I blink up at him, so shocked by the accusation I'm stunned into silence.

Still eyeing me, he reaches for my wrists and unfastens the cuffs, first my left hand, then my right. I push myself up but realize I'm still bound at the ankles, so I'm forced to lay and wait for him to set me free. A thousand reasons why I should protest flit through my mind, but I can't reasonably grasp a single one. When my ankles are free, I swing myself off the bench and whip around, no longer giving him access to my scorched ass. I glare at him.

He lifts a brow. "You've got something to say? Or do we need another round with my paddle?"

"You—I—I don't even know what to say!"

"*I'm sorry,* would be a good start."

"You just—*spanked* me!"

He nods. "Yes, we've covered this. I did *not* spank you for vandalizing my car, because I'm not sure you're up for taking the kind of spanking that would require."

Oh. My. God!

"What!"

"So we'll still deal with that in a traditional, though not quite as old-fashioned, way."

I blink. "What… what method might that be?" I'm almost afraid to ask.

He smirks, his lips quirking up at the edges. "The method we already agreed on, Ms. McAdams. In which I get an estimate for the damage and you pay me back."

That makes me feel stupid. My cheeks heat. "Oh. Right." I clear my throat. "Well, I'm not sure if your old-fashioned methods involve assault, I'd ever want to experience *that* again."

He purses his lips. "Right. You know, you've worn out your welcome here, Diana. It's time to go."

And for some reason, that stings.

But I have to save face. I storm toward the door. I'll die if he suspects his manhandling has turned me on. I need to get the hell out of here and go home. "I don't need your help. I can get home on my own."

"*Stop.*" His deep command freezes me in place, and once more I feel the responding twinge in my belly, my panties dampening. Oh *God.*

I clear my throat. "Excuse me?"

"I'll take you home. I need to contact the rest of my staff and notify them that I'm leaving." Before I can protest he waves his hand and the man I saw earlier with the spiky gray hair and tattoos along his neck walks over.

"Boss?"

"Axle, need assistance. I have a guest I need to take home. Make sure we follow protocol tonight, and tomorrow we have an all-staff meeting with Zack. Got it?"

The man he calls Axle nods.

"Much appreciated."

Axle heads toward the bar.

Cabs are easy enough to get, or an Uber, but it would cost me money I don't have, especially now that I have to pay for the *stupid* repair for the *stupid* car I keyed.

Tobias joins me and grabs my hand. "Don't fucking care if you wanna hold my hand. I wanna be sure you don't go running off and do something else stupid, so you'll hold my hand."

The nerve!

"I can't believe you talk to people this way."

We make it to the door and he opens it, allowing me to go through. "You haven't seen anything yet. If you were mine, I'd have you bare-assed on that bench, lecturing you to kingdom come, giving you triple what you just got, and you'd apologize to *Master* Tobias before I let you dress again. Princess, I'm takin' it easy on you."

I can hardly believe men like him still exist, let alone thrive, and I'm just about to breathe out an indignant huff before I realize that won't get me anywhere, and I need a ride home. I don't have time to wait around for a taxi. I need to get home to my son.

"Thanks for taking it easy on me," I finally say. I try not to let the sarcasm show. "And yes, please, I'll take that ride home. I need to get home as soon as I can."

"Where do you live?" he asks.

"Not far from here." Chad and I live in a tiny apartment nearby. Though I earn a decent income, I'm still at entry level and saddled with student loans. His dad hasn't paid child support in six months, and I don't have a lot of wiggle room in my budget, especially now that I have to pay the babysitter more than I'd planned.

And now I'll have to find a way to fix his car. I groan.

Why couldn't he own a beat-up pick-up or something? Oh, right, I wouldn't have been stupid enough to key a truck. I was so hell-bent on revenge after drinking myself silly at the bar with Beatrice, I desecrated a car worth more than the building I live in.

"Car's out front," Tobias says, then his lips quirk up as if he just remembered something. "Oh, that's right. You're very familiar with where my car is."

I huff out a breath. "Glad you're amused. I, on the other hand, feel like smacking myself."

"Nah, babe," he says. "You don't beat yourself up. No smacking yourself." He grins. "I've already done that for you, anyway."

"Thanks," I mutter, and my ass tingles at the memory. Jesus, the man can swing a paddle.

As we head to his car my phone buzzes. I groan when I realize it's my babysitter.

Will you be home soon? He's awake and scared. The fire alarm beeped and it's freaking him out. Panic shoots through me. The fire alarm? But then a second message flashes on the screen. *No fire. Batteries need to be replaced.*

Thank God. I look up and realize we've made it to his car. My stomach churns as I look at the awful scratch marks that gleam in the light of the moon. Wow, I totally did a thorough job. For a moment I wonder to myself, what would it feel like if someone had done that to my car? All things considered, maybe he *was* taking it easy on me.

But when my ass hits his leather seat, I think otherwise.

CHAPTER 6

I WATCH as she winces slightly when she sits, and I stifle a smirk. Good. The little brat ought to feel a good sting when she sits down after the small, but firm, paddling I gave her. I'd taken it easy on her. Zack would've lectured the hell out of me for not reporting the vandalism. It *had* been an accident, sort of, but the deliberate disobedience hadn't been. Still, after the last smack landed and I no longer saw red, I wondered how she'd react until she mouthed off.

Then, I was glad I'd spanked her ass.

I slide into the driver's seat. Jesus, the sight of her belly-down over that bench, her gorgeous curves on display... if she were mine, I'd have done more than spank her fully-clothed ass.

"Where am I taking you to?"

"Hawthorne and Maine." With a nod, I punch the address into the GPS, and pull onto the busy street.

"How's your son?" I ask. I hope mentioning her son will maybe bring a little peace between us. I don't expect her to look out the window and refuse to answer. I wonder if she heard me.

"Diana?"

"He's… okay," she whispers, her voice catching. "Fire alarm went off and it freaked him out, but the text was from a little while ago. Hopefully he's settled now."

I nod. Has to suck, knowing your kid was freaking out, and you weren't there. But seriously, how's a woman who looks that damn good old enough to have an eight-year-old kid, anyway? I figured the conversation was over, so it surprises me when she talks again.

"You have any kids?"

"No. Divorced, though, so I've been there, done that."

She laughs mirthlessly. "Yep. Me, too. And maybe you think it's weird I'm freaking out over an eight-year-old who'll miss me if he wakes up, so I might as well just tell you, my son's… got some issues." Her voice catches at the end, but she clears her throat and squares her shoulders.

"Oh?" I take a left and slow as we near a stoplight.

"Yeah," she whispers, turning to look back out the window. I won't pry. "Understood." I try to speak gently. Mamas are bears with their children, and I've seen how feisty she can be. I don't want to push her away, or somehow discourage her from talking about what she obviously needs to talk about. As a dominant and owner of Verge, I've got some experience handling highly-charged situations. I'll give her the space to talk as much or as little as she wants. "Got a nephew on the spectrum. Teen, now. Awesome kid. Makes killer calzones. But yeah, he's had his fair share of challenges."

"Yeah," she whispers. "So has Chadwick."

"Like, say, having a name like Chadwick?" As soon as I speak I wonder if I'll touch a nerve, but she rolls with it.

"Hey!" She laughs, then groans.

"Just pullin' your leg, babe."

"No, it's fine. It was the pretentious ex that named him.

Turns out it was a family name, and it was expected we use it. So, whatever. I call him Chad. His father can call him Chadwick."

I grin at her. "Atta girl."

She shifts in her seat. "Thanks," she says, the edge returning to her voice. She's reserved and a little pissed-off again. Jesus, her moods swing like a fucking pendulum.

"How's your ass?" I gently remind her of what her attitude can get her.

"Perfectly toned, thank you, Pilates." She glares.

"Nice evasion."

"I didn't evade anything! You stretched me out on a spanking bench."

"Annnnd we're back to square one."

"Here's my apartment coming up, Tobias. Please pull over here. Thanks for the ride."

I pull up in front of where she tells me to, a worn-down complex surrounded by tall buildings. Diana opens the door despite the fact that I'm opening mine at the same time. She doesn't know how I like to do things, so I don't blame her. I'm a little on the old-fashioned side, and I like to be the one to open the door for a woman who sits her ass in my passenger seat. But as she walks up the stairs near her home, I follow her. I need to make sure she's okay before I leave, the memory of what Zack told me earlier haunting me.

Diana looks with surprise over her shoulder, her hazel eyes curious and something else. Pleased?

"Did I leave something in the car?"

I shake my head, feeling a little sheepish. Has she never had someone watch over her before? "No, just makin' sure you get upstairs all right is all."

"I'm fine, Tobias." The ice returns to her voice then, as she puts her hand on the door knob to her home.

"No doubt you can handle yourself," I reply. leaning back

against the rail. "But you weren't involved with the conversation I had with the NYPD tonight."

Her eyes cloud and she shakes her head. "I did overhear a few things."

"Let me walk you upstairs?" Her eyes shoot to the curb where my car sits before she turns back to me, and bites her lip.

Her eyes grow troubled, and she says nothing at first, as if she's warring within herself, but then she shakes her head. "No, thank you. Good night, Tobias. Thank you for driving me, and for being so understanding about the... incident involving your car. I'll be sure to contact you in the morning." She opens the door to her apartment building, steps in, and shuts the door behind her, not giving me so much as a backward glance.

I inhale through my nose and exhale through my mouth once, twice, three times.

She damaged my car. She defied me and threw me sass. And yet, there's something about her... something I can't seem to ignore.

It's the spanking you gave her, dumbass, I lecture myself as I walk back to my car, shaking my head. I'm conditioned to feel shit for women I dominate, to get hard making them squirm in pain, to protect them. I'm done with this chick, other than making sure she pays me what she owes me. And she will, or she'll answer to me.

CHAPTER 7

I STAND with my back to the entryway door to my apartment building, my eyes closed tight. I listen as he walks away, not moving until I hear the door to his car close, the engine turning over, and then pulling away from the curb. Swallowing the lump in my throat, I breathe in deeply, preparing myself for whatever Chad needs tonight. I'm spent, though. Exhausted.

"I'm such a bitch," I whisper to myself, tears pricking my closed eyelids. "Everything he did… he was almost *nice,* and I was nothing but a bitch. He must hate me."

I feel a tear roll down my cheek but don't stop it. Shaking my head, I give myself the lecture I need to hear.

You are not a bitch.

It's been a stressful night.

And he's nothing to you anyway.

But no… it's a lie. Since my husband left me, I haven't felt anything even close to what Tobias awakened in me. The arousal, fury, and raw attraction he causes frustrates me because *I can't control it.*

And as I walk up the rickety stairs that take me to my apartment, I can't get him out of my mind. I can still feel the way my body heats at the sound of his voice, still feel the smack of his goddamned paddle on my ass.

And hell if that didn't turn me on.

I shake my head, attempting to clear my mind, but as I hit the top step and take my keys out of my pocket, my phone buzzes.

It's Tobias. *Don't forget to call me tomorrow.*

I frown.

I told you I would and I'm a person of my word. I'll call you by eight.

I *humph* as I slide my key in the lock. Another buzz.

Just reminding you.

For Christ's sake. *Thangks*

Ugh. I type again.

Thanls

Shit! Growling out loud, I type with finality.

THANKS!!!

No need to thank me three times or to yell, but you're welcome.

He sends a smiley face with its tongue sticking out, then *Sleep well, Diana.*

I can *hear* his deep voice bidding me goodnight.

Smiling in spite of myself, I push open the apartment door, and brace myself for whatever awaits me. Thankfully, everything is calm when I enter. Mandy's fast asleep on the couch, her thick copy of *Anatomy and Physiology* half open beside her on the coffee table, her head lolling to the side as she softly snores. I can't help smiling. Mandy is a good babysitter, but she is a full-time college student and babysits for several people in the building. She's often asleep not much longer after Chad goes to bed.

The small apartment's tidy, and I feel a peace settle inside me, the peace I always feel when coming home. I inhale the light scent of cinnamon from the candle on the coffee table—unlit, as Chad freaks around lit candles—and slide out of my heels, sighing with relief. I can't wait to get into my pajamas and crawl into bed. Gently, I nudge Mandy, who sits straight up with a gasp.

"I didn't mean to startle you," I whisper, trying not to wake Chad. "I'm home and just wanted to let you know. Want to spend the night here?"

Mandy often crashes on the couch after babysitting, and leaves for school in the morning.

"Mmm," Mandy mumbles. "Thank you."

"No problem. Night, honey. Sleep well." I lift a folded blanket from the back of the couch, and flick it open over Mandy, who falls back asleep almost immediately.

Sleep well.

A small gesture. A simple phrase. Still, my chest warms at the thought, and I allow myself a brief moment of fantasizing about him saying those words to me while I lay beside his strong, sturdy frame, as he tucks a blanket around me.

It isn't about the *sex*. I just want to sleep *next* to him.

I imagine him yanking his shirt off and stripping down to his boxers, then joining me in bed. My body warms at the thought.

Ok, it's definitely about the sex, too.

I pad down the carpeted hallway to check on Chad, my eyes now heavy with exhaustion. The door to his room is halfway open, as he likes it. He hates having his door closed and needs a nightlight to sleep. The little wand-shaped nightlight is plugged into the wall, illuminating a half-circle behind it, and his soft breathing calms me. Mandy was good to get him back to sleep when he woke. Many nights, he needs me to help him back to bed, or listen to him talk about his dreams, or sit by his side and hold his hand until he falls asleep. His father left us in the middle of the night—packed his bags, and when we woke in the morning, he was gone. Chad hates going to sleep.

Chad's light brown, curly hair falls onto his forehead and pillow, his sweet face at peace in sleep. A well-worn copy of *Harry Potter and the Sorcerer's Stone* lays on the table next to him. I watch as his shoulders rise and fall in slumber. I like how the little worry line between his brow softens when he sleeps. In the morning, he'll be full of questions for me about what I did tonight. But for now, he sleeps, and I'm grateful.

Padding back down the hall, I walk to my bedroom, take out a fluffy pair of sky blue pajama bottoms and a tank top and toss them on the bed, then strip out of my clothes. Exhaustion makes my limbs ache, my eyes are scratchy from lack of sleep. I step out of my panties but before I slip into my night clothes, I walk to the full-length mirror that hangs on the back of my bedroom door. Biting my lip, with a sharp intake of breath, I spin around to get a good glimpse of my ass.

The skin's a bright pink, and there's even a rounded shape on one cheek. A mark from the paddle.

My heart thumps wildly in my chest, even as my mind goes crazy.

Get him out of your mind. He SPANKED you. Only crazy people do that.

Philippa hadn't seemed crazy, and she was definitely a regular. Hell... *Tobias* didn't seem crazy. He's just... stern. Old-fashioned.

It doesn't even make sense that pain makes you horny.

No! God, no, I'm not horny, I lie to myself, turning around to take in my naked breasts, full, with peaked nipples.

He hadn't even kissed me. He'd only spanked me.

I keyed his car! Besides he isn't *boyfriend* material. *God.*

I practically run to the bathroom to finish getting ready for bed.

I will *not* fantasize about Tobias. I will not pull out my trusty vibrator and replay the spanking he'd given me, or fantasize about being tied up, or *anything* like that.

Nope. No way.

But as I close my eyes, the memory of his strong, sturdy, sexy as hell body comes to mind and despite my mental protestations, I find myself fantasizing, my hand between my legs working myself to climax at the memory of the spanking bench, and his deep, commanding voice, before I drift off to a restful, dreamless sleep.

"MAMA? MAMA, YOU AWAKE?"

I roll over, rubbing the sleep out of my eyes, and looking at my tousled-haired son staring down at me.

"Do I look awake?" I mutter in a sleepy growl.

"You do now."

I laugh. "Fair enough. Morning, sweetie."

Chad throws his arms around my neck and squeezes tight. "I missed you last night."

Nodding, I push myself to sitting in bed and yawn widely. "I missed you, too, baby. Did you have fun with Mandy?"

He nods. "We played Uno. I won."

"You always win at Uno."

"Yup. It's because I'm really good at it."

Chad doesn't pull any punches, but states the bald facts.

He tips his head to the side. "What's for breakfast?"

I sigh and close my eyes. "Cereal. Lemme sleep. Ugh, I'm exhausted. What *time* is it, anyway?"

I don't have anywhere to go on a Saturday morning, because I work Monday through Friday when Chad's in school.

"It's seven oh-nine."

"It's still dark out," I mumble, before a bright light and the snapping sound of shades being lifted make me sit up straight in bed.

"Chad!"

He shrugs. "Just making it not dark in here anymore."

"Hmph. Thanks."

I glance at my phone. I told Tobias I'd call him by eight, but now that I'm waking, my stomach churns with nerves.

I don't want to call him.

I won't shirk my responsibility for what I did, but I don't want to deal with the arrogant son of a bitch straight out of bed either.

Ok, so maybe he's not exactly an arrogant son of a bitch. I think of how he walked me to the door and held my hand when I had an anxiety attack.

The memory of him spanking my ass flashes in my mind, too.

Yeah. He's a jerk.

I follow Chad, noting that Mandy is gone, when the door buzzes. Chad goes into the living room and taps the intercom.

"Yeah." Remembering to greet people is a social skill we're still working on.

"Chad," I chide. I'm in no position to entertain anyone. I don't even have a bra on.

Chad looks at me and shrugs. "Hello. Who is this?"

For a brief moment, I panic. Is it him? Would he come back so soon?

"Beatrice here! Lemme up, kiddo."

Chad pushes the button without responding. I go to the

coffee maker, grab a pod from the basket on the counter, pop it in and push the button. I need coffee, pronto.

"You shouldn't drink that," Chad rebukes, standing in the other room with his arms crossed on his chest. "Caffeine is bad for you."

"An uncaffeinated mama is bad for *you,*" I retort. "Trust me. Hazardous to your health," I mutter, as the delicious liquid sputters then streams into my cup. A knock sounds at the door.

"Make sure you—"

But Chad opens the door, and Beatrice saunters in.

"Gotta check who's at the door, kiddo," Beatrice admonishes, side stepping into the room. "My God, Diana. You're still in your jammies?"

She walks over to me wearing yoga pants and a top, a hooded sweatshirt, and sneakers.

"Shut *up,*" I mumble. "You're back from yoga, right?" I take my mug and slosh French vanilla creamer into it, give it a quick stir, then slurp it down. "Ahhhhh." I exhale, momentarily closing my eyes.

"Mama says it's dangerous for me if she doesn't have her coffee," Chad says, going into the kitchen and opening a cupboard.

"Hell yeah," Beatrice agrees, pulling out a chair at the table in the dining area. "Baby, it's better for *everyone* that your mom has her coffee."

"I wish I had a donut," Chad says.

"Me, too," I agree.

Beatrice wrinkles her nose. "I cannot unravel an hour of yoga by eating those things."

I snort, before taking another sip of coffee. I swallow, giving her a look. "You'd rather unravel it with beer. I know, you have priorities."

"Damn right," Beatrice says. "Ok, so…" she looks to Chad.

"Chad, baby, I have a new game on my phone and need some help. I can't get past the licorice swamp level."

Chad rolls his eyes and holds out his hand. "It's all about strategy. Gotta break the cages on the bottom row *first,* before you even look at the pastilles in the top row."

Beatrice shakes her head with mock disbelief. "You're a wonder," she says. "Do me a favor. Break this level, while your mom gets changed and we have a talk?"

He shrugs. "If you really want me to."

Beatrice hands him her phone, and I walk toward the bathroom. "Honey, grab some cereal, okay?"

"Yeah."

He sits on the couch and is already swiping his fingers across Beatrice's phone.

I stalk into the bathroom and grab a plush pink towel, putting it on the counter. "Ok, I know you're here to pry," I begin. "So why don't you just cut to the chase?"

"Diana!"

I snort, running the water in the shower, steam rising in the small bathroom.

"Ok, so. You were… taken into his club. His office. What happened? Girl, this is killing me over here. I hated leaving you there with a stranger."

I grin, stepping into the tub and stripping out of my clothes. I toss them into the basket on the other side of the tub and start to soap up under the stream of hot water.

"He was beyond pissed. And he wanted me to pay for what I did. I, stupidly, thought it would be smart to contact the insurance company, but he reminded me that they will not cover an act of intentional vandalism."

"Oh my God." Beatrice sits on the toilet, her shadow just on the other side of the curtain.

"Ok, so then we go into his club, and I'm still thinking I'm just going to figure out a way for insurance to cover it when he tells me that we'll either make an arrangement for me to pay, or he'll notify his police officer friend, who you may have heard him refer to outside?"

"Yes!"

"And I promised him I'd pay. But then he got all..." I pause, running a razor over my soaped-up legs. *"Bossy."*

"He *got* bossy? Babe, he was born bossy. The only shitty part about this was that you met by keying his damn car. It would've been so much nicer in any other circumstance. He could've been *the one,* Diana."

"Oh for God's sakes, don't start that again. There is no *one.* No one's going to rescue me. So stop it."

Beatrice sighs. "Sorry. Okay so you went into the club and gave him your number?"

"Then his police officer friend called. It seems there was a sexual assault victim last night."

"Thank you, NYC," Beatrice moans. "When isn't there?"

"Well, there's a problem though. Someone from the club supposedly instigated this or something."

"His club? What kind of club is it?"

I feel my cheeks flush, and it isn't just the hot water. "A BDSM club," I say in a rush.

I can hear Beatrice's audible gasp even over the sound of the water.

"Oh my God!"

"It gets worse."

"How can it get worse? Girl, you keyed the car of a... *dom?"*

I giggle in spite of myself. "Yup."

"Did he... what did he do to you?"

"Well, nothing for the car incident." I soap up my arms and chest, wondering if it is wise to tell Beatrice, but I *have* to. "But, um... we had to go into the club... And I got super curious. So while we waited during the investigation, I got another member there to give me a tour. Against his instructions. And he was... not pleased."

"How not pleased?"

"He may have... *spanked* me." The outrage returns. "He spanked me!"

"Well, if he asked you not to go, and you did anyway..."

"Beatrice!"

"What? Facts are facts."

"I'm a grown woman."

"A grown woman who acted like a child!"

"Whose side are you on, anyway?" I squeeze the loofah aggressively and soap my legs with vigor.

"*Yours,* babe." I squeal when the curtain pulls back and Beatrice stands in the gaping hole, letting the cold air hit me. "Turn around. I don't wanna see your tits, I need to see if you're still marked."

"Beatrice!"

Beatrice just glares and twirls her finger around to indicate she wants me to show her my ass.

"For *Christ's* sake," I mutter. "No privacy!"

"None. I wanna see."

Shaking my head, I show her my ass, weirdly proud of the marks I bear.

"Oooh," she says. "Your ass *is* sorta pink, like you've been spanked. There's even like this half-moon shaped mark. You always did have a nice ass." The shower curtain shuts, and Beatrice resumes her place on the toilet seat.

"I can't believe you just did that."

"Eh, we've seen each other naked hundreds of times. I can't believe *you* keyed the car of a *dominant,* then disobeyed him in *his club,* and got *spanked."*

I sigh and shut the water off.

"I am *so* jealous."

"*What?*"

"I am! I want a spanking. I wanna be dominated," her voice pitches off into a whine.

"It wasn't like that. He just... humiliated me," I say, grabbing the towel. I towel-dry my hair. "It wasn't *sexy.*"

"Honey, if that man orders *coffee,* it's sexy."

The memory of how wet I'd gotten the night before from just remembering the way he put me over the spanking bench in the club makes me squirm.

I shake my head. "Anyway, yeah, a night for the books. And now I'm supposed to call him today and figure out how much I owe him." My voice catches at the end.

Beatrice stands, comb in one hand, my bottle of Super Curl in the other. She spins the comb around, instructing me to let her at the curls. No one can tame my curls like Bea.

"Aw, babe." her voice is soft and soothing. "Maybe it won't be so bad."

"Doesn't damage to a car cost... like a shit ton of money?"

"Well... maybe he'll get a deal?" Beatrice says helpfully.

I just sigh again, my head tugging back as Beatrice combs through my curls.

"Maybe," I whisper.

"Listen, babe. You've paid your share of shit dues. You've been handed the *worst* luck of anyone I know. Between your string of asshole exes, your miserable excuse for a father drinking away your inheritance in a move destined to break records in liver destruction, losing your job at Markell, and..." her voice trails off, and neither of us needs to hear the last stroke of bad luck.

"Chad isn't bad luck," I whisper. "He just... needs a bit more."

Beatrice hugs me from behind, her voice thick with

emotion. "I didn't say he was. I was gonna say the Yankees losing in the World Series last year."

I laugh, even though my eyes cloud with tears. Sure, she was.

"Yeah. I could use some good luck," I say with a nod. "But some days, it's all about working your ass off, and has shit all to do with luck."

We both jump as Chad pounds on the door. "Mom! We are out of the cereal with red berries. And why are you two in the bathroom together? That's super weird."

I can't help but snicker. "She's just doing my hair, honey," I yell. "I'll be ready in five minutes."

"I need cereal now. I hate that shredded wheat stuff. I'm starving!"

I feel my nerves rise. "Chad, *wait.*"

"My stomach hurts I'm so hungry."

I turn away from Beatrice, needing this conversation to end. I push open the door to the bathroom. Not a lot can make my son happy, but one thing that always does is a frosted donut.

"We'll go to Tulio's and get a donut. Okay?"

My phone vibrates. I pick it up, and glance at the message.

Just checking. That eight o'clock phone call? That was eastern time, right?

I grin, flushing a bit, before I respond. *Sorry, my son needed me. Will call soon!*

I like toying with the Big, Bad Dom.

I quickly pull on jeans and a red sweater, a thin but warm one that dips a bit low in the front and hugs my curves, then fluff out my still-damp hair, and quickly dab a little makeup on. Just a touch of foundation and gloss, but for today I also run a mascara brush through my lashes.

I never wear mascara. And it has nothing to do with the

fact that I'll likely meet up with Tobias or something. *Nothing.*

Pulling on a pair of low-heeled boots, I imagine him frowning at his phone, and a part of me feels a twinge of guilt, but not enough to call him. The idea of speaking to him again… no, I can't do it. Maybe I can resolve this whole thing by text.

I pick up my phone. Another text from him.

Define "soon."

I can *hear* the deep, corrective tone in his *text.* My heart flutters a little, and I'm just about to respond when a loud pounding sounds at my door.

"I'm *starving,* mom."

"Okay, okay, I'm coming," I mutter, ignoring the demand on the phone in favor of the demand on the other side of the door.

When I open the door, Chad's glaring at me. "Why did you take so long?"

"I was getting ready. Now stop being so selfish, Chad. You want donuts, I'm getting you donuts."

"I'm starving!"

"You are not starving. Children in third world countries who have nothing to eat but rice are starving. And if you're that hungry, we have plenty of food here you could've eaten."

He quiets, and Beatrice gives me a sympathetic look. Sometimes I feel like I get it from all sides, people telling me I spoil him. And maybe I do, a little, but I feel responsible for his father leaving us. Beatrice knows better than to give me that lecture. I don't really *spoil* him, per se. But I know he struggles with things not being the way he expects them, and I want my kid happy.

The three of us walk to Tulio's together. Icy wind whips at my hair and cheeks, and I pull my coat tighter. God, it's freezing out, and snow is on the way.

The scent of cinnamon and sugar and coffee fills my senses when we arrive, and I inhale deeply. I *love* this place. It's been around since I was a kid. It's the place my daddy frequented and yeah, my dad had been an alcoholic who couldn't hold down a job, or pay his bills, which earned righteous scorn from Beatrice, but despite what people said, he'd loved me. And this place had been special. Just ours.

My eyes feel heavy from lack of sleep, and the thought of the phone call and expenses I face make my nerves churn. I need more coffee, stat, and a chocolate donut. As I take in the sight of frosted cakes and cookies, and the small line of customers ahead of us, Chad goes up to the window that houses the donuts, and I watch as his back goes rigid.

Crap. Rigidity is often the prelude to a meltdown. My breath catches in my throat

"Chad?"

The customers in front of me finish placing their orders, and I go up to the counter to order as Beatrice walks over to Chad. "What's up, honey? Find your donut?"

"No," he responds, far louder than necessary.

Aw, *shit.* I clear my throat. "I'm sure they have vanilla frosted somewhere, honey," I say hopefully, flashing a big grin to the cashier. "Right?"

The teenaged girl shakes her head sadly. "Sorry. We sold out this morning and won't have any more until tomorrow." The smile freezes on her face when she sees Chad's hands clenched into fists by his side.

"None?" I try. "You can't... make some more?"

The girl's face falls. "So sorry. We can't, no."

Okay, alright then. "I'll have a Boston cream for me, and an extra-large coffee with an espresso shot."

And Bailey's, too, I think grimly.

"No Boston cream either."

Well for fuck's sake.

"Chocolate covered?" I turn to look at Beatrice, hoping we can come up with a solution, but there's no such thing as a solution where Chad's concerned. He digs his heels in, wants what he wants, rigidity one of his many challenges. He can't handle seams in his socks, his chair moved out of order at school, a substitute teacher, or a *strawberry* frosted donut when he's expecting vanilla. I inhale deeply, then exhale. Beatrice shakes her head and puts up her hands in a helpless gesture. "No idea," she mouths.

The door to the bakery jangles, and before I even turn, I *feel* him. The now familiar scent of power and grace and masculinity envelopes me.

Can this morning get any worse?

I turn my head just to confirm that yes, indeed, Tobias stands behind me. He blinks in surprise. So this is as much as a surprise to him as it is to me. At least he's not following me.

I smile. "Morning. We were just... ordering donuts."

He gives me a smile that doesn't quite reach his eyes. "Morning. Clearly. Go on, don't let me disturb you." He gestures to the counter. The sarcasm makes my stomach clench. And *God,* why does he have to look so damn good? He wears black boots and a long-sleeved, olive-green t-shirt that stretches taut against the large expanse of his chest, the color accentuating his swarthy skin. The t-shirt's tucked into his jeans at his narrow waist, his hands astride his hips.

I clear my throat.

"I want a vanilla-frosted donut," Chad says. "Nothing but vanilla."

The girl at the counter looks abashed and merely shakes her head. "We have lemon?"

Chad's eyes cloud, his hands still clenched in fists. "I *hate* lemon."

"We could go home," Beatrice suggests, "and pick up some of that cereal you like on the way?"

"Mom said I could have a donut." Chad's voice is barely controlled, rising in pitch. My son is gonna have a meltdown, right here where Tobias can see. *No.*

I try again. "Honey, we've established that they don't have the one we want."

Chad growls. "I want vanilla!"

"Wouldn't get that kid a donut," mutters an elderly lady exiting the shop. "In my day, kids weren't so damn spoiled." My cheeks flush, my chest hot and tight.

"Whoa, now." I hear Tobias's deep voice behind me. Oh, no. He is *not* stepping into this.

He speaks with authority, his voice calm. "They don't have vanilla, kiddo. But you know what I order? I like the glazed bow ties. It's a very manly donut. Don't you think? Bow ties and all?"

Chad blinks up at Tobias and his mouth parts open a little.

I watch in wonder.

"A bow tie?" Chad repeats.

"Mmhmm," Tobias continues in his deep voice. "They're bigger than the other donuts and perfectly glazed here. I highly recommend them. But like I said, they're kinda... *manly.*" He frowns a bit. "You think you're man enough to handle that, though?"

Chad looks to the counter, then back to Tobias, and back to the counter again. "Of course I can handle it," he finally says.

I blink. Seriously?

"I'll take two bow ties," Tobias says over my head. "Add her order to mine."

"You don't need to—"

His sharp tone cuts me off. "Go find us a table, Diana."

Swallowing hard, I remind myself that he has good

reason to be pissed. We need a table. No, I won't *cow* to the bossy man. It just makes good *sense* to do what he says.

"Fine," I say, sputtering a reluctant, "Thank you."

"I'll be going now," Beatrice says, her eyes doing a quick but chaste once-over of Tobias. She nods approvingly, winks at me, and *leaves. The jerk.*

Tobias pays for our order and without meeting my eyes, orders, "Table."

CHAPTER 8

NORMALLY I DON'T TAKE TOO KINDLY to people not following through with promises. I suspect her failure to call me has more to do with nerves than evasion, but it's still not cool. She's lucky she's so damn beautiful and has somehow bewitched me a little. I knew I'd track her down eventually.

Thankfully, the universe agrees with me, and on a day when I'm craving a glazed Tulio's bow tie, she practically falls into my lap.

I'd get her there. And when I did, she wouldn't be sitting upright. Apparently, I didn't do a good enough job the first time I spanked her.

After handing cash to the cashier, I toss a tip in the jar in front of the register, grab her enormous cup of coffee and our box of donuts, then head over to the table where Diana and her son sit. Her son eyes me curiously, Diana's eyes flit about the room, not meeting my gaze.

I pull out one of the wrought-iron chairs and sit down heavily, flicking the tape on the white bakery box, and pull it open. "One bow tie for you," I say, handing it to her son. "One for me, and one chocolate for your mom."

"Say *thank you,* Chad," she instructs her son.

"Thank you," Chad says around a huge mouthful of donut. The boy has his mother's beautiful hazel eyes but his hair is lighter, finer, and slightly long and a little curly. He wears a pair of jeans and an Avengers long-sleeved t-shirt. He eyes me thoughtfully as if trying to figure out who I am. He looks like he's inherited his mom's spunk and beauty. I like him already.

"Chad, this is Mr. Creed. Mr. Creed, this is my son, Chad."

I extend my hand to Chad, who stares. "Tobias," I say. "You can call me Tobias. You know how to shake like a man, Chad?" Chad blinks and Diana starts sputtering, but I ignore her and plow on. "Put your donut down," I tell him. Learning how to shake like a man is a lost art, one that I was taught. Shaking hands properly shows character and conviction, and before I think about what I'm doing, I'm demonstrating. I watch as the boy puts down his donut.

"Now extend your right hand and take mine in yours." Chad's gaze comes to mine as our hands meet. The boy barely grasps my hand, his small, cold hand enveloped in my larger one. "Firm, Chad. A man has a firm handshake. You look the person in the eye, and shake like this." I demonstrate.

Chad follows my example. "Good job," I praise. I won't look at Diana. If she's pissed, she can keep that to herself because *I'm* pissed.

"So, Chad, your mom and I met last night." Chad nods, taking large bites of his donut. "And she was supposed to call me this morning. Turns out, I didn't have to track her down because, as luck would have it, I stumbled upon her in the bakery. Isn't that lucky?"

"Mmm." Chad's preoccupied eating. "Lucky. And this manly donut *is* yummy."

Diana smiles at him. "I swear I can see hair growing on your chest already."

Chad's eyes widen, and she laughs out loud. "Teasing, baby. Teasing."

She turns to Tobias, no longer smiling. "So. Are you sure it was by *chance*?" she asks, her beautiful hazel eyes flashing.

"Totally, babe. Stalking isn't one of my strong suits." I shoot her a tight smile. The nerve. "No time for that sh—" I look to Chad. "Ahem. Stuff."

She rolls her eyes. Christ, the woman needs a good, hard session, preferably over my knee.

"Talked to a buddy of mine. Owns an auto body repair shop. Says he'll do the work for me at cost. But I have a proposition for you."

She freezes with her coffee cup at her lips, her eyes wide and curious. "Oh?"

"Can you get a babysitter again?"

She nods. "Yeah, and every other weekend Chad's dad has him."

Ah. So there's a father in the mix.

"You want to take my mom on a date?" Chad asks, taking another large bite of his donut.

"Hoping for dinner."

Those curves. The fiery eyes and quick wit. Yeah, I'll maybe forgive a few hundred dollars for a chance to get to know her better, and I suspect under any other circumstance, she'd flat out refuse to date me.

"I don't date men like you," she says, sniffing, turning away and sipping her coffee. Though her tone is disdainful, her body turns to me, her chest rising rapidly as she inhales and exhales, and I note that she grips her coffee cup more tightly.

"Figured that," I say. "So that's why this isn't a traditional date request. I want you to understand exactly what I'm asking you. Come on a date with me. We find a way to wipe your debt clean. We move on."

Her eyes widen and her mouth drops open. I feel my lips twitch. "Get your mind outta the gutter. Not *that* kind of a repayment."

"Just dinner?" she asks.

I shrug. "Dinner, maybe dancing, maybe drinks." And a good, hard spanking, delivered in the method that will show her I mean what I say, but leave her wanting more.

She clams up, her lips shut tight, before she finally parts them and whispers, "I don't dance."

"Fine, then. Just dinner, on me." Despite the fact I'm telling myself I need to make sure she pays me back, something in me tells me not to let this woman go. I haven't met someone like her, so feisty and so desperately in need of submitting, in *decades,* possibly ever. She wars with what she wants, like fighting for air to breathe, and it's the battle within her that draws me to her. She's into this. And I'm not giving her a taste of the lifestyle and leaving her to someone else. *I* want to be the one that explores this with her. I like the challenge… The chase. The capture. Fuck, my dick hardens just thinking about it.

So she has a son, and one with special needs. Already, I like the kid.

The quote Braxton gave me for the damage was easily half what I'd expected, and since Brax owes me a favor, most of it will be covered.

Now it's time for me to capitalize on meeting *her.*

I get to my feet. "Pleasure to meet you, Chad." I make a fist and reach out to fist bump the kid. "Bump the fist, bro," I say, demonstrating. Diana tenses and opens her mouth to speak but before she does, her kid tentatively bumps my fist with his own. I smile. I feel like somehow, I've won something, but I have no idea what.

"Diana? See you at seven tonight."

She blinks, swallows, and finally agrees, "Seven."

"YEAH?"

I take the call from Zack just as I open the door to Verge. It's several hours before we open, but I need to get paperwork done in the office.

"Another attack, man."

"Fuck. Already?"

"Yeah," Zack blows out a breath on the other end of the phone. "Witnesses says the man mentioned Verge. Seems too obvious for it to be a member, though. I mean, who goes around assaulting women, dropping club names?"

"Right." I slam the huge, metallic entryway door, spin on my heel, and stalk to my office. "She survive?"

A pause, and then, "Barely."

Fuck.

A part of me wishes the perpetrator *is* a club member, so I could have the sick bastard alone in one of the private rooms. I'd teach the motherfucker a lesson, and he wouldn't be sticking his dick into some unwilling chick, making what's supposed to be an act of love a disgusting act of violence anymore.

"Be careful," Zack says. "I've screened every one of your employees, all have solid alibis for the first night. Not sure a member isn't somehow involved, though, and I'm not sure why anyone would mention your club at all. Especially if they *are* a member. So just… be cautious. Warn your team, and keep a close watch on things."

"'Course." I'm already on it. We have protocol in place to notify each other of suspicious behavior, and I'll do whatever it takes to keep my shit tight.

Zack pauses. "So Brax tells me some chick keyed your car."

"Brax needs to keep his fuckin' mouth shut."

"Couldn't be helped, man. Tia needed some work done, took her in, recognized your car. What'd you do to get your car keyed?" Tia is Zack's younger sister.

"Didn't do anything. Keyed my car by accident."

Zack's low whistle makes my lip twitch. Any dominant I know would have something to say about what she'd done.

"Heard you spanked her ass. You think that was enough retribution?"

I huff out a laugh. "Not for keying the car, no." I should've known. Stretching the girl out on the spanking bench and paddling her ass isn't something that would fly under anyone's radar. Especially a girl wearing red heels instead of the common black leather and latex members donned. She'd stuck out like a sore thumb, and people had noticed.

I still don't regret it.

"You'll work it out," Zack says.

"See you tonight?" I ask?

"I'm off duty so yeah," Zack says. "Let you know if anything else changes."

We disconnect, and I boot up my laptop, pulling up member profiles. Though I like to believe that a member of Verge isn't responsible for such a horrendous act of violence, the evidence concerns me. Frowning, I scroll through one profile sheet after another. Verge draws a large spectrum of members, being situated in the heart of NYC, just blocks away from the Financial District. Members are required to be twenty-one years or older, and all are subject to background checks. Still, I don't know each of the four hundred plus members personally, as only twenty or so percent frequent the club on a weekly basis.

Our staff is solid. Verge isn't just a BDSM Club and bar,

but a function hall. Beyond the private rooms we host high protocol parties and munches a few times a month. The income generated from the parties and munches alone sustains the upkeep costs of Verge. Took a while, but my partner Seth and I are now drawing hefty salaries.

I'll be damned if I'll see our work go up in flames because of some asshole who belongs behind bars. No fucking way.

After scanning through over half of the member profiles, not surprisingly finding nothing at all that clues me in, I flick off the profiles and click over to the business software. Two hours later, after bills are paid up-to-date and correspondences caught up, I shut the laptop and run a hand over my eyes and the bridge of my nose before standing and stretching.

My stomach growls. I haven't had anything to eat since breakfast with Diana and her son earlier this morning. Pushing to my feet, I grab my phone and scan the messages. One from Seth.

Gotta be sure expenses are up-to-date. Rochelle and I are returning from New Hampshire this weekend. Want to do it then?

I quickly fire off a response. *All set. Caught up this afternoon.*

Another one from Zack I'd missed earlier, and several emails. I swipe the notifications off the screen. An incoming message pops up as I push past the door to my office and into the hall that leads to the club.

Diana.

So... realizing this sounds like the most dumbass question I've ever asked... does a dom have... rules for dates?

I can practically hear her husky, sexy voice. I grin, my fingers traveling quickly over the screen.

That's a very good question. There is only one problem, though. We haven't discussed rules, consent, or hard limits. I'm not your dom unless we scene, and we don't scene unless we discuss those limits.

No response comes for a minute as I make my way to the lobby, and then the bar. Though the place is vacant, it's warm and welcoming, my home, and I take it all in with pride. The bar with the overhead lighting is beautiful enough to grace the cover of a magazine, the seating in the bar area welcoming and comfortable. There are no windows in the main room, though we've taken pains to bring in a few accoutrements that one might find in a regular bar. Two large pool tables sit in one corner and there's a circular dance floor complete with a disco ball. During open club hours, dance party music filters through top-of-the-line speakers.

My phone buzzes.

Didn't seem to bother you the other night, though. You spanked my ass without any... formal consent.

I smirk.

Wrong. I asked you. We didn't do contracts or hard limits but you did consent.

Oh. Haha. Right.

A pause, then, *So no rules for tonight?*

I stare at my phone. She's pushed her limits with me many times now, but she enjoys the attention. My dominance. My dick twitches as I look down the darkened hall that leads to the private rooms, and the dungeon where I spanked her ass. I love rules. I thrive on control. Always have. I've been into the scene since a former girlfriend brought me to my first party.

I'll take it easy on Diana. But what's the point of a date if you don't have fun?

No panties.

I imagine her squirming wherever she is, maybe biting her full, beautiful lip, and I hope the panties I've just forbidden are good and soaked.

Ahh. Okay. Oooh, dirty.

Does she think this is just a game? I frown before responding, *The correct response is Yes, sir.*

A full beat passes before the phone buzzes once more.

Yes, sir.

Good girl. You are all set for tonight?

Yes. Chad's dad will get him at six, and I'll be ready by seven.

I'll be there.

I shove my phone in my pocket and walk over to the bar, remembering how she sat perched on a stool sipping her water. I check the taps and bottles, making sure the trash has been emptied, and the store of salted nuts we serve warmed is full. Verifying that the fridge is stocked with lemons and limes we'll slice later that evening. Clean glasses line the bar like soldiers at attention. I open the large plastic bag filled with laundered, folded bar mops, place a neat stack on the designated shelf beneath the counter, and tuck the rest away in the cabinet. Leaning back against the bar, I take a moment to enjoy the quiet, to take in the solitude, my chest rising and falling with the deep, cleansing breaths I take.

I grew up in one of the most run-down neighborhoods in New York, my mother taking care of me and my four younger siblings on government assistance after my father left. We lived on Top Ramen and food pantry handouts. Part of me wishes I could show my mom what I helped build, where my hard work has landed me. The prestigious, beautiful private club renowned across the country as one of the best clubs on the East Coast. But now my mama rests comfortably in a nursing home, paid for by me and my siblings, surrounded by her crucifix, her rosary between her fingers, and visited weekly by the local chaplain.

All my mom knows is that I'm a successful businessman and run a business. She doesn't ask questions; I don't provide details. Her bills are paid, and I donate to the kids' hospital in her name. I keep her happy and well provided for, and she doesn't have to worry about a thing. That's good enough for me.

I make the rounds. The pool tables have been brushed and covered, chalk replaced. The dance floor is polished and ready. Then my pulse quickens as I make my way to where the real fun happens, thoughts on Diana. I eye the array of toys that have been sanitized and readied for tonight—the spanking implements on tables and affixed by hooks to the walls, ranging from moderate floggers to severe canes. The violet wands and Wartenberg wheels, aimed for careful sensation play. Members frequently provide their own sensory deprivation hoods and gags, the more experienced of our members.

Once I assure myself the rooms are well stocked and clean, I inspect each private room and glance through the list of reservations. The indigo room is still vacant tonight. I smile to myself. I'll keep that in mind.

CHAPTER 9

I STAND in front of the full-length mirror in my bedroom. Chad's with his father, and the nervous feeling that always flutters through my tummy when I'm separated from Chad doesn't dissipate like it normally does. Even after a stiff drink, the butterflies only seem to flutter faster.

"I can't believe you texted him that shit," I hiss to Beatrice. "Honest to God, I don't have a dominant bone in my body, but I could beat your ass with my bare hands."

I'd been in the bathroom when Beatrice took my phone and texted Tobias, and when I caught her red-handed, and read the texts she'd already sent and his responses, I wanted to *die.*

"No panties. Great. Just *great!* You are *unbelievable."*

She only shrugs. "You'll thank me later."

"For *Christ's* sake," I mutter, opening up my underwear drawer and glancing wistfully at the contents. "Now if I wear them he'll probably… spank me or something." My heart stutters in my chest at the thought.

How would he check?

"Honey, you need to *live* a little," Beatrice says, taking a sip from her coffee mug. "You've done nothing but date boring ass *attorneys* and *doctors* and guys who… *shave* and stuff."

In spite of my anger at her, I huff out a laugh. "You say it like it's a stupid thing to do."

"Babe, you need a *real* man. A guy with hair on his chest, not one of those little pansies who talks all night about *investments* and the stock market and the benefits of high-protein diets." She wrinkles her nose up in disgust, and I shake my head.

"Some very nice men shave and eat high protein diets," I protest.

"Exactly. That's my *point.* I wanna see you do better than *some very nice man.*"

I frown at my reflection. "You sure the little black dress will do for a BDSM club?"

She shakes her head. "You don't even know if he's taking you to the club, do you?"

My heart sinks a little at the possibility of him *not* taking me, and that's how I know. Damn, she's right. I don't want a *very nice man.* I want a guy who knows how to live a little. Maybe someone who's a little... dangerous.

Tobias drives me absolutely mad, but I *like* being the sole focus of his attention.

I slide into the little black dress, and Beatrice stands behind me, zips it up, and leans in and whispers in my ear, "You've set your sights too low, babe. Set them higher. You need a guy who can handle your fire sign."

I roll my eyes. "You know I don't believe in that sign crap."

Beatrice shrugs. "You don't have to. I know who you are. Stubborn and feisty and strong-willed."

I slide on a pair of silver hoop earrings and sniff. "Thanks."

"And loyal and kind and you have the biggest heart of anyone I know," she continues.

I swallow hard and don't reply, picking up a small glass bottle from the silver tray on my dresser and spritzing my neck and wrists, rubbing them together. Next, I walk to the bathroom to apply my makeup, but just as I twist the brush off my tube of mascara, the door buzzes.

"Oh my God! What time is it?" I ask, my stomach doing a somersault.

"Oops. It's seven on the dot."

"It's him! Stall!"

"Me?" Beatrice squeaks. "You want *me* to stall the big, bad dom?"

"He's not going to blow your house down or anything."

Beatrice wags her brows. "No, but maybe he'll blow *yours* down."

I groan, shaking my head, laughing in spite of myself as I began applying the eye makeup. "*Bea, go.*"

She runs.

"Hello?" I hear from the bathroom, then I hear Tobias's baritone reply. Seconds later, the door buzzes while I blot my lipstick, and just as I pucker my lips and perfect the look, a knock sounds at the door. My heart stutters a wild beat in my chest, my belly dipping as I hear Beatrice fumbling with the lock.

"You don't have a chain?" he asks as way of greeting.

"Oh, well, I don't live here," Beatrice replies. I stifle a groan. "Diana will be right out. May I get you… a drink or… something?"

So. Classy.

I give myself one last look, slide into the silver heels I'd set out to wear, and go to meet him. When I come around the corner, he's leaning against the dining room table, facing away from me. I can see his profile. My belly warms as I take him in.

He's wearing slim-fitting black pants with a white button-down shirt tucked into his waist. His narrow waist widens to broad shoulders. His dark hair is slightly damp, and he carries his jacket on his arm. He's so beautiful, I forget how to speak and only stare, suddenly shy.

That's when he sees me. His eyes heat, taking me in, doing a quick but appreciative once-over. The heat between us crackles, and suddenly, in my mind's eye, I'm pushed over the bench at Verge, my ass perched in the air, and he's behind me, stern and ready to punish me. He reaches for my hand. "Diana." His deep voice reverberates through the room, the mere sound drawing a low throb between my thighs. The way he says my name makes me feel like royalty.

I can only nod, not trusting my voice.

"Ok you two kids, have a great time!" Beatrice chirps from the kitchen. "And, um, make sure you have her home by midnight, young man." She wags a scolding finger.

I groan. "For God's sake," I mutter, but Tobias only grins.

"Can't promise I'll have her back by curfew," he says, wordlessly taking the coat from my hands and holding it for me to slide into.

The formal, gentlemanly gesture makes me feel bashful. "Thank you," I whisper, slipping into the coat.

"You got a hat and gloves?" he asks. "Cold as Siberia out there."

I nod, removing them from my pocket, while Beatrice nods approvingly from the kitchen. He leans in, a lip quirking up, his obsidian voice washing over me. "Didn't know we'd have an audience. Would've inspected to be sure you followed instructions, but it'll have to wait until we're alone."

Electricity zings between my legs at his words when I

realize what he means. *He's going to check if I have any panties on.*

I swallow hard, hoping that whatever plans he has for me tonight include alcohol of some sort that would, *please God,* numb my vanilla sensibilities. He takes my gloved hand in his, and waves to Bea. "Night," he says, opening the door to my apartment. Standing beside him, I feel somehow smaller, younger. Attractive.

I will not cave, I decide. *Will. Not. Cave.* He's just a guy. There are no "Mr. Rights." There is no man who will be my savior. I'll never rely on another human being to give me what I need. I'll never let a man sweep me off my feet again. I need to protect myself.

"You like Italian?" Tobias asks.

"Love Italian. There's literally like no such thing as an Italian dish I won't eat."

"Calamari? Tentacles and all?"

"Mmmm. Yum."

He grins. "Ok, so I need to swing by Verge after dinner. You game?"

I'm suddenly tongue-tied, the idea of going to Verge as his *date* does strange, scary, wonderful things to my lady parts.

Damn, I'm hopeless.

"Cat got your tongue?" he asks. I shrug and bite my lip, shaking my head. I can't reply. My mind is a sudden jumble of confusion and hope and heat.

His lips twitch. "Didn't mean to intimidate you, honey. But gotta tell you, not happy with a lack of response when I ask you a question." He pushes the button for the elevator and turns to look at me. "We're new, so I should explain to you that I expect an answer when I speak to you. So I'll ask you one last time. Cat got your tongue?

God! I swallow. "No."

His gaze sobers, just as the door to the elevator swings open, we step on, and as the door closes, he whispers in my ear, "No, *what?*"

Oh, God!

"Um, no, sir," I say, finally remembering the text conversation. Beatrice and those damn texts. I'm half-tempted to tell him the truth but it's too embarrassing. And if I'm honest, calling him *sir* is oddly titillating. A reminder of his authority or something. I've never in my life called a man sir.

Until now.

"Very good," he says. A surprising warmth floods my cheeks and chest at his praise.

After Chad went with his father, I'd spent some time surfing the web, finding groups on Tumblr and Fetlife, watching YouTube videos that made my jaw drop in shock, or cringe in horror (*Knives? Breath control? Hot wax?*) while others made me shift on my chair with arousal at the very *thought* of Tobias doing some of those things to me. But one thing that made the longing in my chest grow was the complete and utter control that submissives gave their dominants. To reach that level of trust, you'd have to let yourself stand at the threshold of pain and know that the person you granted authority and control to would not hurt you, but protect you. Care for you. Make you the sole focus of their attention.

And though I don't consider myself a selfish person, I have to admit, being the absolute pinnacle of another person's focus is utterly compelling.

I want that.

"You're deep in thought, Diana." The timbre of his voice, low and mellow, snaps me out of my reverie. I merely nod. He slips a hand into his pocket, and takes out a shiny copper penny.

"Penny for your thoughts?"

"That's so corny." But I can't help but laugh.

His lips twitch, his eyes crinkling around the edges, and the look makes my belly warm again. He sobers as the doors to the elevator open and we exit. "You don't want to talk about what's on your mind?"

"Maybe after a glass of wine?" I venture, cringing as I see the still-demolished door of his Maserati. I hope he'll allow me to drink. I wonder. Is that a thing? Not allowing drinks? I remember his admonition and his not allowing me to drink at Verge, but that was a different circumstance.

"I can arrange that."

THE REMAINS of my Caesar salad with grilled shrimp sits in front of me, and I sip the last drops of wine from my glass. It's delicious, but I don't ask for the name. I'll never afford another glass.

Maybe it's the wine that makes him seem so much... *sweeter* than I'd initially thought. His cool, calm, collected nature does something to me, giving me the idea—no, the hope—that this is a man to be trusted. Conversation flows easily. He speaks of his home life as a child, the oldest of four kids in the Bronx, with a stern, tough-as-nails single mom who'd made him toe the line.

"Do you see her often?" I ask. He nods.

"Once a week and on holidays, my brothers and sisters visit, too. She's a good woman and likes where she lives. Holds the cribbage cup title, runs the book club, and sometimes sneaks into the kitchen to bake pies." His eyes soften, talking about his mama, something I sorta love. "They let her, but she doesn't know it. And you?"

I look away, my throat tightening at the thought of talking about my own childhood. My father who I loved but who never did pay the bills, and my mom who put out, so she could. No, I don't want to talk about them. Not now. Not yet. The only people I want to talk about he's already met. Chad and Bea are the ones who matter among the string of those who've failed me.

"Let's table that convo for now," he says, his warm, strong hand reaching out to gently rub the pad of his thumb over the top of my hand. The gesture is sweet and somehow soothing, and my pulse quickens at his touch.

"Ready to divulge what you were thinking about earlier?" he asks. He sips from his frothy, dark beer, his level gaze focused on me. "Something tells me it has to do with our going to Verge later. It's the only reason I'm pushing it."

"What?"

"What you were thinking about earlier."

I look away quickly. "My mind is like a squirrel or something, you know. Hmm, what's for dinner. Oh, I need stamps! Did I sign the permission slip? Damn, I think I left a load of laundry in the dryer downstairs. Did Angelina Jolie break up with Brad Pitt, or vice versa, and what the hell kind of child support does he pay?"

His shoulders shake with laughter. "Point made," he says. "But I don't believe you forgot what you were thinking about."

Damn. He's good.

"Do they give you, like, mind-reading skills in dom school?"

He nods seriously, though his lips twitch. "Among other things."

The napkin I pick up and finger is a cream-colored brocade, edged in crimson stitching that likely matches my cheeks. Inspired by the wine and the easy, comfortable conversation, I'm feeling braver. "Do they teach you to… tie girls up?" He fills my wine from the bottle on the table, and I gratefully take another sip, the sweet liquid warming me through. My eyes flit back to him, and his own gaze, though heated, is slightly amused. "And do they teach you to—to use those—wand things?"

"Violet wands? Maybe."

"What about..." I bite my lip and my heartbeat quickens, my breath traveling through my lungs as if labored and half-frozen, "like... pain and stuff?"

"Spanking?" he asks outright.

A jolt of shock courses through me. He just... *says* it... like this is *normal.*

I swallow a gasp and pretend to be all brave about it, nodding silently. I don't trust my voice.

God, I'm such a wuss.

"So bondage, yes. Violet wands, I learned from a former master whose skills are unparalleled. I've learned wax play and sensory deprivation. But to be honest," he says easily, as if we're talking about baking cookies or changing a tire, "a submissive really teaches a dom how to spank. I know how to wield a paddle. I can bring a sub to sub-space with nothing more than a flogger. I don't favor caning but can give a caning that doesn't injure, or a strapping that teaches a good, solid lesson." He pauses, and finishes the rest of his beer in several long gulps before finishing. "But a good spanking is most effective when administered with honest feedback from the submissive.

Hearing him speak like this, I feel my naked pussy clench between my thighs. Fire creeps along my neck and collar-bone. If just hearing the man talk about... all these things... turns me on, what would it be like to *experience* them?

I suddenly noticed our waitress standing next to him, her mouth gaping open. She blinks when we look up to her, then mumbles something about hoping our meals were good, before she turns tail and runs away.

"Scaredy-cat," I say, finishing my wine. "Not sure why a little spanking talk is so outlandish."

He grins, a full, wide-tooth grin that lights his whole face like sunrise over the ocean, making me smile back easily.

Something about pleasing him makes my belly flip with pleasure.

God, he's hot.

I lean across the table, spurred on by my attraction to him, the wine helping me leave my inhibitions behind, and whisper, "I did what you said. About my clothing... or... lack thereof. Are you going to check, sir?" I shiver when his warm hand caresses my knee, gliding upward softly, bringing heat along with his touch. He lifts the hem of my dress and grazes just one finger along my inner thigh. My whole body tremors.

He growls, his eyes molten, his voice husky and low. "I'll get the check."

I SIT on the passenger seat of his car, clenching my thighs together. I've made out with men and been less turned on than I am after eating a single dinner with Tobias.

"Glad you obeyed my instruction," he says in his low voice. "I like that, Diana."

My name spoken in his deep, reverent tone, makes my chest tingle with pleasure, my skin prickling at the possessive sound of it.

Get a grip, girl, I lecture myself. *You can't develop a crush on a guy who owns a BDSM club. No crushes allowed.*

But as I look over at him, his large, powerful frame easily navigating his car through the congested streets of NYC, another thought flashes through my mind.

Why the hell not?

I know why not and can enumerate the reasons easily, as I have in the past. Chad's counting on me. I can't go around losing my shit to some guy I barely know. Again. Falling for a guy means I could get rejected, and I fucking hate rejection. I can't do that to myself.

I know now, no man will ever deliver me from the shit hand I've been dealt, and I almost don't care anymore. I've got good friends, a son I love more than life itself, a fulfilling job. Happy endings are meant for the pages of a book. I've worked my ass off making a good life for me and Chad, and I'll be damned if I'll sink to the level of expecting some guy to make me happy.

So when we come to a stoplight and his large, warm hand rests on my thigh, his fingers lightly graze the naked skin where my dress rises, I freeze. The wine has begun to wear off and with it, my courage.

I have to ignore the way my body flames to life at his touch.

He tenses, and asks in a low tone, "Do you want me to remove my hand, Diana?"

There's my name again. *Shit.*

I swallow. "No," I say out loud. My mind tells me to get a fucking grip, but my body thanks me.

His fingers grip my leg tight, a warning that both surprises and arouses me. The correction makes my nipples furl against the fabric of my bra.

"Try again."

What? Oh, right.

"No, sir."

Once more, calling him *sir* brings with it a flush of pleasure. Swallowing, I say no more, silently cursing the roller coaster ride that careens at a breakneck speed.

Yes. No. Don't stop. Stop!

More wine at Verge is a must.

He approaches the intersection that brings us to Verge, and slows the car to a stop, giving my leg a little pat. "You'll find that I like control."

Yeah, no kidding.

He continues. "Time will tell whether or not you enjoy allowing me to have it."

I don't know how to respond. I want so desperately to give him control, to see what it would be like to have someone else tell me what to do, if only to satisfy my curiosity.

"We're almost at Verge. Follow my lead. You and I need to have a frank discussion that I'd prefer to have in a private room."

I feel my eyes go wide, and his chuckle makes me blush. "Don't worry so much. I just want to talk. Okay?"

"Okay. Yes. I mean Yes, sir."

He squeezes my leg appreciatively. "Good girl."

God, I want that hand somewhere else. My pussy pulses with the need to be touched. I barely stifle a whimper when he removes his hand to park the car.

"Stay there. I'm coming around to open your door."

Obediently, I wait for him, swallowing hard as he comes around to my side of the car. Where did this guy come from? He's like some kind of throwback from a simpler time. Well… minus the whole kink thing.

My hands shake with nerves.

The car door opens, and he takes my hand, helping me out onto the curb. He tucks my coat around me and pulls me up against his side. "It's cold. I'm glad you wore a warm coat and not that shell of a coat you wore yesterday."

"I don't like bulky coats."

"I don't like frostbite."

Alrighty then. I tuck my head, grateful for the wall of protection his large frame offers as the wind whips my legs and the bare skin of my neck and cheeks. Opening the door to Verge, he half-lifts me in, bringing me in from the cold. A burly guard stands at the door, defying the bitter cold by wearing nothing but a t-shirt stretched tight against his muscled chest and arms, dark, worn jeans, and black boots. It's like the Verge dress code. He has a shaved head and a strong, chiseled jaw with a thin beard that's vaguely familiar. He's huge, and looks ready to take down the Hulk if need be.

"Hey, Geoff," Tobias greets. "Meet Diana."

Geoff gives me a chin lift. "Met last night. Philippa was giving her a tour."

Ah. Geoff's the *Daddy* dude I met in the dungeon.

Tobias nods. "Right. Geoff, you hear anything from Zack?"

"Nope. Tell you this, anyone touches my girl, not gonna be held responsible for what I do."

"No shit," Tobias says. The large metallic door shuts with a bang behind us, bringing with it a feeling of finality.

I'm here with Tobias in his Club. As his date.

As his... submissive?

Am I?

"Got some things to check on," Tobias says, reaching for his phone. "Later, Geoff."

"Later."

He swipes a finger across the screen and I see the name *Zack* come up. He hits *send* on a text, then puts his phone back in his pocket before he takes my hand.

I don't remember the hall being so dark and long last night, and I shiver as I walk beside him. "Cold?" he asks. He places an arm around my shoulders to warm me, tucking me up against his side as we walk. The immediate protective gesture makes sudden tears spring to my eyes.

Girl, you're a mess.

I want to shake myself. I'm falling, hard, and it seems

every time I fight against it, he does something to draw me back in again. I'm not quite sure I like the loss of control.

As we near the end of the hall, a door opens, and a couple comes in. The man, like Tobias, is tall and intimidating, with a shaved head like the guy at the door but leaner, more muscular, and clean-shaven. The curvy, vivacious blonde woman by his side is clearly his, holding onto his hand as their arms entwine. She wears a silver choker about her neck.

A short while ago, I wouldn't have thought twice about her necklace. Now, after spending time perusing all things BDSM online, I know better. She's a collared submissive. They're long-term. A quick glance at her hand reveals a thick silver wedding band on the ring finger of her left hand. Ah. Married, too. So people do take this beyond casual scenes.

"Hey, guys," Tobias greets. He stops and gestures to the man. "Diana, this is my partner Seth and his wife Rochelle."

Rochelle looks from Tobias to me, a smile playing on her lips. Her light green eyes warm as she reaches for my hand. "Pleased to meet you," she says pleasantly, her long blonde hair swinging freely. She seems skeptical but welcoming, and I instantly like her.

When Seth takes my hand, he speaks less enthusiastically. "Diana," he says with a curt nod of his head. "First time guest here?"

"No," I say, not exactly sure how to respond. "I've been here once before." The last time, I wasn't a guest but I did get my ass paddled, so what does that make me?

"Hear anything from Zack?" Tobias asks, clearly changing the subject.

Seth shakes his head and sighs. "No, man. Wish I did. Need to end this shit before it gets out of hand."

Rochelle speaks quietly. "Two injured, Seth? It's already out of hand."

He looks at her sharply, but she stands her ground. "I know what you mean, honey, and I'm not contradicting you. Just saying, this was out of hand the first night."

His jaw clenches. Geez, some of these guys have authority complexes. But then, with a nod, he agrees. "That's a fair point." He turns back to Tobias. "We're heading out for the night. All good on the main, little scuffle by the bar but Travis nipped that in the bud. Brax is monitoring in the dungeon, only one private room in use, and all else quiet."

Tobias says good-bye as Seth and Rochelle take their leave. They're like soldiers reporting for duty, briefing each other on the status of their watch.

As we continue to walk down the hall to the bar, Tobias explains his philosophy. "This is more than just a club," he says. "If I ran a normal club, I'd do the normal things. Check to make sure we have supplies, bills are paid, the atmosphere is welcoming. I'd make sure members are happy, and I'd see what we could do for marketing and the like." He stops outside the door to the bar. "This is different. We do not advertise. We do no marketing of any kind. Members come here strictly by word of mouth. They're vetted and approved on a one-on-one basis. My staff undergoes rigorous training and background checks. We ask a lot of them, and we pay amply in return." He pauses a moment, turns to face me, placing a finger under my chin. I swallow and focus on not moving my gaze away from his, the reminder to focus on him makes my breath catch.

"What goes on in this club is highly charged, Diana. We call it Verge for a reason. Members who come here to play are on the verge of so many things, and it's our job to fulfill their needs. Emotions run high. Danger is always present and flirting with danger can be hot as hell. Gotta make sure it doesn't veer into real danger. And this week, thanks to some asshole who gets off on violating women, two women have been victims of sexual assault and somehow my club's name is involved." His jaw clenches. "I take the running of this place very, *very* seriously."

I swallow hard. "I'm glad you do. People should feel safe in a place like this." His protective attitude resonates with me.

Caveman, my mind protests.

So what? I protest back.

He nods, and to my surprise, he leans over and places a gentle kiss on my forehead, making my belly warm, and a tingle spread along my neck, before he tugs my hand and leads me to the bar.

The room is far busier than it had been last night, both pool tables are occupied, and nearly every seat at the bar taken. Three bartenders pour drinks at breakneck speed. "Drinks are limited," Tobias says. "Alcohol can enhance the experience but dims the senses, and we don't like to encourage members to over-indulge."

"Makes sense," I say. "So what's my limit?"

"You're with me, so your limit will be determined by me," he says.

Really?

"What if I don't like that?" The snap in my voice takes me by surprise. He turns to me, both brows raised, his face a mask.

"Excuse me?"

"What if I don't like that… restriction?" I push.

His jaw tightens. "Seems we need that private talk sooner than later."

He lifts a hand to greet the bartenders, who all nod to him, and as he walks, people sit up straighter, a low hum of interest buzzing through the crowd. A woman who'd been jostling her friend and laughing turns sober at the sight of Tobias. His presence commands respect.

Somehow, inexplicably, the way his power affects others makes my naked thighs damp with arousal. *God!* Yet my nerves churn as I look toward the private rooms. I don't regret my question. It was an honest one, and I'm within my rights to ask. I agreed to go on a date with him. Thanks to Beatrice's shenanigans, I am sans panties, and I've called him *sir* on several occasions. Still, knowing he is going to take me to a private room makes my mouth go dry and my legs go wobbly.

"Travis," Tobias greets, with a signature chin lift. The bartender I met before, with the slow, easy drawl, gives him a chin lift back in greeting. "Had a situation?" Tobias asks.

Travis pulls a beer and slides it on the bar to a man who waits, wearing a leather vest over his bare chest. I bite the inside of my mouth, stifling a grin. Fascinating choice of attire.

"All handled, boss," Travis says. "Couple 'a doms gettin' too big for their britches by the pool table. One thought it proper he bust the ass of a sub with the pool stick." Tobias growls, a low hum I feel in my lady parts. "Brax stepped in and stopped that on his way to the dungeon. Dumbass number one comes up to the counter and orders a drink, dumbass number two comes back and words got heated, started shovin' each other like a buncha pre-schoolers on a fuckin' playground. I pulled 'em apart and called Geoff to give the men their escorted exit."

"Who the fuck was it?"

"Some local professor, if you can believe it. And the other guy I didn't know, Brax said he was a regular but hasn't been here in a while."

Tobias nods. "Travis, you remember Diana. She's with me tonight. We need some time in a private room. You need anything, you call Brax or Geoff, they need anything, call me. Otherwise, I'm off duty the rest of the night."

"You got it, boss."

Tobias wraps a possessive hand around my elbow, his firm touch making my belly dip for the millionth time tonight. He holds me with conviction and ownership, the very touch making me feel more alive than I have in years. "Shit gets hectic after ten," he says in my ear. "Better get you to some privacy before it gets too rowdy in here."

Well then.

We move past the crowd and continue to march toward the private room, passing by the dungeon. Out of the corner of my eye, I can see the place where he spanked me, and my ass clenches with the memory. I swallow hard and keep stride with him.

"Private rooms aren't reserved for just anyone," he explains. "Only long-term members are allowed reservations."

"Makes sense," I say in a rickety voice. "Then why are you taking me? You don't know yet if *I'm* someone who practices safe, sane, and consensual."

He smirks. "Because I run this place, I can already read you, and…" he pauses, taking out a set of keys from his pocket and sliding a large silver key into the lock. He pushes the door open, giving me a small smile, "…it's my job to keep things safe and sane. And you granted me the consent in spades."

I can't look him in the eyes. It's too embarrassing.

He takes my hand and points to an overstuffed chair in one corner of the room. The lights are dim but a lamp on a table flicks on when he hits a switch inside the door. "Go to the loveseat and wait for me."

Is this how it'll be now? He issues commands and I obey? Or does he just act like this when he's in Verge? Am I just supposed to listen to him and nod like a little puppet?

Frowning, I do what he says and perch on the edge of the loveseat.

I hear him behind me, straightening things out and examining the contents of the room before returning to me. I look around the room. In one corner is a huge, king-sized bed with a curtain surrounding it, and what looks like a very sturdy headboard with circular rings attached in each corner. I swallow, my eyes traveling to a bedside table with a black velvet bag laid on top, and in one corner of the room, I see a small, opened doorway, but I can't see beyond it. A desk flanks one wall, with a high-backed wooden chair pushed up against it, and on the desk a silver tray sits laden with matches, feathers, and something else I can't quite identify. A tin of mints or something? A huge fireplace sits exactly opposite the bed, and to the right of the fireplace, near to where I'm sitting, is a black leather recliner with a pile of fluffy blankets. I blink. The room is gorgeous, clearly meant for an extended stay of some sort, and decked out for all sorts of… fun. I can see why only seasoned members are allowed entry.

I continue to take in every detail—the burgundy walls, framed prints edged in gilded silver, a soft stream of music filtered above me, a low, melodic blend of instrumental music. I watch Tobias slide a remote onto the desk where he stands. He picks up the matches and strikes one. The room soon fills with the scent of fire and vanilla. My legs tremble, as if watching him prepare the room is some sort of foreplay. He takes our coats and hangs them on a hook in a small closet, then I watch as he shrugs out of his suit jacket, hangs it on the back of the chair by the desk, and makes his way over to me.

He sits on the other end of the loveseat, so close our knees are touching. "Do you have any questions, Diana?"

I swallow, rubbing my damp hands on my thighs, and

look about the room. "I have so many I'm not sure where to begin," I whisper.

"Start with the room," he suggests. "Look around and ask me anything that might make you curious." I look around again.

"Ok, well, for starters, what's that tin on the desk?"

"Those are strong peppermints. I like to use them in situations that get intense. The mints have a calming effect."

"Oh. And why such a large pile of blankets? This room is warm but small, and that pile seems excessive."

"Sensation play is a very real kink for some of our members. One of those blankets is made to aid in sensation play. One side is soft and velvety, the other rougher. Also, submissives can sometimes drop after a scene—they might be cold, in sub-space after a session. The blankets help regulate body temperature."

I feel my eyes go wide. "And the... the rings on the bed posts?" I whisper. Clearly, I haven't been reading the right websites or something.

He smiles. "Those rings are used for a variety of purposes. I use them to hold restraints, mostly, as a modified whipping post. I like my submissives to be restrained if it's going to be an intense session."

My breath comes out in a shaky whisper, and I swear my womb convulses. "Whipping?"

Without blinking, his face sobering, he nods. "Yes."

"I don't know if I'd like that."

"And that, Diana, brings us to why I brought you here."

My heartbeat kicks up. He brought me here... why? Suddenly, I realize what a foolish thing I've done. If he tries to take advantage of me, how would I get out? We're isolated. The rooms are sound-proof.

"And," I clear my throat. "Why would that be?"

"Because we need to have a talk. In the lobby or foyer area

before we get to the bar, couples are encouraged to talk about limits, consent, and safewords before they ever enter. I didn't do that with you since I had no interest in scening with you, until you defied me."

Hearing his words makes me squirm uncomfortably on my seat. "Oh?" I clear my throat.

He nods, still sitting a good distance away. "Yes. But now that we're here, and you've shown an interest, there are things we need to talk about."

"Like what?"

"Like what interests you and doesn't. What your hard limits are. What things you'd want to try and what things you wouldn't?"

I swallow, wishing I'd gotten a drink from the bar. "I… I'm willing to try… anything… *once.*"

"Okay then. For now, you have the house safeword, which is the name of the club. I go too far, you say Verge, play immediately stops."

"Got it."

"Really willing to try anything?"

"Well yes. Maybe not the hardcore pain stuff… yet? Even if it's something that I don't find arousing or interesting, I'll try it. I mean I had no idea I'd get turned on by getting spanked, but there it is."

"Did you?"

"Did I… what?"

His voice lowers, his eyes heating. "Get turned on."

I swallow. "Well, yes. Doesn't everyone? I thought I was normal or something. At least based on what I read online."

He smirks. "You can read anything online to convince you of whatever you want to hear."

I frown and pull away from him. "What's that supposed to mean?"

"Hey, you don't have to get defensive. Basically, means

that yeah, some people get turned on and some don't." His eyes sober, and he crosses his arms on his chest. "And I wouldn't have asked you on a date if I didn't know with certainty that you are the kinda girl that does."

Both embarrassment and a sort of pleasure flood me simultaneously, and I'm not sure how to respond. "You mean —you wouldn't—be *interested* in dating me if I wasn't a girl who got off on spanking?"

He shakes his head sharply. "Of course not."

"What? That's ridiculous."

He frowns. "Why is that ridiculous?"

"Because there are so many perfectly… reasonable… healthy women out there who are *not* into this, or so you say yourself, and you wouldn't even give them a chance?"

"Diana." His voice is patient but stern. "In case you haven't figured it out by now, I'm the kinda guy that gets off on control. I'm the kinda guy that gets off on power. I have no interest in pursuing a relationship with a woman who isn't able to fulfill that need of mine."

Fulfill… a need. *And oh no, wait. Pursue a relationship?*

I let that sit for a minute.

"Any other questions?"

"What's in the velvet bag?"

"It's filled with tools. Handpicked implements and other things I wanted to have on hand."

I feel my jaw go slack. "How did you pick them?"

"I placed an order," he says with a shrug. "I have people who work for me."

"What made you think that I wanted to… play… with any of those things?"

"You said yes to a date. To a date with a man who identifies as a self-professed dom."

"Maybe I just think you're cute."

His eyes wrinkle at the edges. "Maybe. My gut says otherwise."

"Are you always right?"

"Most of the time."

"How arrogant."

"Not gonna argue otherwise."

I look around the room once more. "And the door. What does it lead to?"

"A fully equipped, very comfortable bathroom should the need arise on any level."

"I see."

My chest rises and falls while I breathe in and out. I take deep, cleansing breaths so I can think clearly. "Okay, so… I have a very pressing question that I can't hold back anymore. It's important, Tobias… sir."

He nods soberly. "Yes?"

"How am I… how can we… proceed with any type of relationship if I owe you money for what I did?"

He nods slowly. "And that's the other reason I brought you here tonight. I wanted to offer you a proposition."

My thighs clench together, already knowing that the proposition has my interest. "Oh?" My voice is a husky whisper.

"Yes. I got the estimate for the damage to my car."

I listen, not wanting to interrupt. He continues. "I'm afraid to tell you the cost." In a rush of words, he tells me.

I close my eyes briefly at the number. "That's half of what it would've cost otherwise," he explains, "But that's the best they could do."

It will take me a year or more to pay him. It will take *forever.* And I'll have to skip the vacation Chad and I are planning for spring break. Maybe sell some of my things.

"What's your proposition?" I whisper.

"You may pay me in other ways."

Was he thinking what I was?

"Like… sexual favors? I'm not that kind of girl, Tobias, and if you think that —"

"And *I'm* not that kinda guy, babe." His jaw tightens once more. "Not sexual favors, no. But I'm going to give you the chance, tonight, right now, to make amends for the damage against my property. I'll punish you. And once we're done, we'll consider your infraction wiped clean."

My breasts swell, and I shift on the couch to hide the arousal that courses through me at hearing him say *punish you.*

"How will you punish me?" I whisper, looking back at the ominous bag that sits lifeless on the table.

"Over my lap," he says, patting his knee, the gesture making my squirm. "With my hand. You behaved like a child, so I'll punish you like one."

"So I don't have to like, suck your cock, or something like that?"

His eyes narrow, and he literally growls.

"Okay, okay," I say. "So how long do I have to think about this?"

"Offer stands indefinitely. Pay me back if you want. Or lie over my lap, and take your punishment. I don't care if you wait six months and pay me halfway then decide to pay off the remainder with your ass."

"Well, that's fair enough," I agree amicably, then, "no *wait.*"

He waits.

"Do we get this in writing or something?"

"I can do that if you want."

His implacable patience unnerves me. Does the man ever lose his cool? Well, other than when a drunk chick is keying his car… he was pretty impatient with me then.

"Okay, then, alright," I agree, nodding.

His eyes widen in surprise. "You've decided?"

"Yeah," I say. "I'll—I'll take my punishment. And when I'm done, my slate is clean?"

"Exactly."

A little spanking and I'll pay off the debt? It's a no-brainer. The last spanking he gave me wasn't *that* bad. Plus, the idea of straddling Tobias's sturdy thighs appeals immensely. It's not like he's putting me in the stocks or anything. Getting over his lap would be hot.

At least in theory.

"You're… not gonna spank me with anything more than your hand?"

His lips twitch. "You sound disappointed."

"I'm not!" I lie, my thighs damp with arousal. I swallow hard.

His low, commanding tone makes me shiver a bit. "Just my hand, babe."

I stand in front of him and no matter how hard I try to stay calm, I shake, my whole body trembling though it's warm and comfortable in the room. He leans forward and takes one of my hands. "Don't be afraid, Diana."

"But it'll hurt," I whisper.

He nods. "It will. But it isn't something to be afraid of. Yes, sometimes, it is. But at other times, you'll see it's a gateway for a lot of things. And when you stand up after having taken your spanking, you'll know you did it. That you're brave, and strong…" his voice trails off and grows husky. "And maybe a little turned on."

Turned on? I'm already ready to spontaneously combust.

He looks into my eyes, and his voice softens a bit. "Let's get this over with." He pats his knee. "Come on, now. Over my lap."

My whole body teems with an electric vibe of nerves and arousal and excitement as he guides me to one side of his lap, then gently pushes me belly-down. When my stomach hit his knees, I freeze with apprehension. Maybe this wasn't such a good idea. Maybe I can pay him back somehow. Is this some sort of game to him? My cheeks flush at the mere thought.

"Wait!"

His large hand rests on my ass, and the intimate gesture makes me squirm. I'm so damn aroused, the heat of his head seeps through my clothing.

"Yes?"

"Am I too heavy?"

"Of course not."

"Okay, then."

I feel him raise his hand.

"Wait again!"

He lowers his hand and sighs.

"What is it?"

"I—is this—are you tricking me?"

His body shakes. "Tricking you? How exactly would that work? You're belly-down over my knee about to get your ass spanked. I've spanked you once before and now it's time for another spanking. When we're done, you have my word that your debt is wiped clean. What part of this might be a trick?" He shakes his head again, and the heat on my cheeks intensifies.

"Are you laughing at me?"

He wraps a hand around my waist and lowers his mouth to my ear. "I am not tricking you. I am not laughing at you. You're cute. What I am doing is getting impatient." His tone sharpens, and I suddenly became very, very aware that I'm in the presence of a dom who likes things done on his terms. "You agreed to be punished, now stop fighting it and take what you're due, or I *will* spank you with more than my hand. Understood?"

I nod. "Yes. Yes, sir. I'm sorry."

"Good. Now before I begin I need to be sure you followed my instructions."

Ahhh! He's going to check!

I feel the hem of my dress rise, and cool air sweeps across my naked ass. A warm, sensual caress of his hand on my bare skin makes my breath catch, and my pussy dampen.

"Very good," he says approvingly. "That's what I like. Jesus, Diana, you have a gorgeous ass."

"So I'm told," I whisper, my eyes close tight in apprehension, arousal, and excitement. "Again... Pilates."

"I'll have to find this Pilates," he growls, running a hand over my ass again and again, "And thank him for his magic."

I giggle. "You can be really goofy for a stern guy, you know that?"

"Goofy?" he asks, and to my shock, he slides a finger through my slick folds.

"Oh!"

"Jesus Christ," he swears reverently. "You're soaked, baby. Fucking *soaked.* And I haven't even spanked you yet."

"Is that normal?"

"Normal? Fuck yeah. But Christ, girl, you undo me." He probes my channel with firm, confident strokes that make me whimper with need, before he gently, expertly, flicks my hardened clit. "Someone's ready to fly," he rasps. "I don't ever want you to wear panties around me. I need access to this pussy. For tonight, this pussy's mine."

A whimper escapes as he withdraws his fingers and I could cry with the loss.

"I told you I'd spank you, Diana. And there's something you need to know."

I shut my eyes tight, my hands tucked under my chest as I brace myself for the punishment. I can only nod. "Mmm?"

"I always do what I say I will. *Always.*"

His palm cracks down on my ass with a sudden sharpness

that takes my breath away. I reel from the pain, the intensity of flesh on flesh jarring. Another sharp smack followed by another. He builds a slow, steady rhythm, paying attention to every single inch of my naked skin. I lose count after ten, and still he continues, fast, hard, stinging smacks. I'll never need an *implement* or whatever those things are they use at the club. His hand is plenty effective.

How long will he spank me? How hard? Will I bruise? My mind is a slew of muddied questions as I buck and rear on his lap, but he holds me fast against his knees.

This isn't for pleasure, though. I'm being punished.

"What you did last night was impetuous," he says. "Vindictive, yeah, but you likely had your reasons. You should've checked that it was the right car. You should've been more careful." His corrective tone makes tears spring to my eyes as he continues the torrent of smacks. "If you'd done that to another guy who was less forgiving, I hate to think of what could've happened to you."

Another barrage of smacks land. My ass is on fire, but my pussy even more so, it's aflame with what I so badly need from him. "I'm sorry," I squeak out, my voice thick with emotion.

"Good," he says, with another sharp smack. "Five more, and we're done here."

Five more. Ok, alright. I can do this. I brace myself, needing this to be over. I can't take this anymore, not just the pain but all of it. The emotions that consume me, the loss of control. My need to come, come hard, and come *now.*

He lifts his hand and smacks it down with a sharp *crack* that resonates throughout the room. A second swat follows the first, then another, until all five spanks are over. I sag against his lap when he stops, my ass fiery hot.

"You're forgiven, now," he says.

"Thank you," I whisper, not even quite sure what I'm

thanking him for. A sort of peace comes over me. And as I lay over his lap, totally spent from the experience, a part of me wonders what it would be like to have this the norm. To pay for my sins by taking a punishment that makes things right again. Yeah, I'm an adult, but… can it really be that simple? Can I trust him that much?

"You took that spanking like a good girl," he says. "I'm told my hand spankings can be severe."

"I don't have a reference point," I whisper. "But that was no cake walk."

He chuckles, then his hand strokes my pussy once more.

"Open," he orders, a harsh command that takes me by surprise. Obediently, I part my legs.

"Fuck yeah," he growls. "This pussy's so fucking sweet."

"Mmm," I mumble, not caring that I've just been spanked in the middle of a BDSM club. *What would my mother say?* I need the release only he can bring. I'm delirious with arousal.

"Please… sir," I beg.

"Please what?" He responds with an upward stroke that makes me arch my back.

"Let me come," I rasp. "Please… let me."

"Right now?" he asks, pumping two fingers into my channel. My heart stutters a crazy beat in my chest, my entire body an electric hum of need.

"No, tomorrow," I quip, earning me another blistering smack, before he returns to my pussy, stroking my clit hard and fast.

"Wiseass."

"*Sore* ass," I groan.

"Good. Ah, that's a girl," he encourages as I push my pelvis against his hand, writhing with every stroke of his fingers. "Good girl."

I sob as my need rises, until I know I'm going to lose my mind, and tumble into ecstasy. "Go ahead, Diana," he allows.

"Come now. Come when you're ready. Let me make it better."

Rapid strokes of his fingers make me buck, my body so tense it hurts until finally, *finally,* I plunge over the edge. I hear a guttural moan then realize it's my own voice. He holds me and strokes me until I peak, then just when I think I'm coming down, another, sharper, more intense orgasm rides the first.

"Oh, fuck yeah," he says. "My baby comes in multiples. Yeah, that's what I like to see. Greedy little pussy. Sweet, greedy little pussy that likes to come." His words somehow make me climax even harder. After what seems forever, I collapse.

What the *fuck* just happened?

Pulling down the hem of my dress, he turns me around on his lap. "Sit up, honey."

I sit up on his lap, feeling drunk with arousal and pleasure and pain. My ass burns hot, my sex still throbs from the intensity of my orgasm. I slump against his chest, welcoming the sweet protection of his arms around my shoulders. I burrow in close, shivering a bit.

"Intense, huh?" he asks.

"I wasn't prepared for that," I whisper. I hardly know the man and yet I need him to hold me. He does, pulling me up against his chest in a tight cocoon, as if he knows this is what I need. I feel him tense slightly as he reaches up and snags the folded blanket at the back of the couch, snaps it open, and folds it over my shoulders. The extra warmth is just what I need, and my eyes slide shut. "I could go to sleep like this," I whisper.

"If you want to, that's okay," he whispers back.

My eyelids feel heavy, my body boneless. "Terribly fascinating first date. Dinner, spanking, sleep. I'm just… so tired. I'm sorry."

"You don't need to apologize. I've enjoyed your company."

"Yeah? You liked spanking me?"

"I'd be lying if I said I didn't." I feel something hard against my ass, and I realize there is more than retribution in that spanking he gave me. He's turned on. The knowledge makes me smile despite my exhaustion. Yeah, I like turning Master Tobias on.

I force my head back. "I don't understand all this, you know."

"I know."

I like that he doesn't try to offer any platitudes or explanations. "This—attraction to you. The turn of events. How pain can make me so damn horny."

His lips twitch, and yet he lets me speak unhindered.

"There are things here that scare me," I whisper.

His arms tighten just a notch around me.

A slight catch in my throat makes my voice come out wobbly, but I have to say it before the moment is lost. "Just about the only thing that *doesn't* scare me… is you."

He weaves his hand through my curls, a possessive grip on the back of my neck, and he leans in. He's spanked me now, twice, and made me climax as many times, but I know he's going to kiss me now. Butterflies dance in my stomach and I hold my breath.

His lips meet mine softly at first, questioningly, asking permission, and when I grant that with parted lips, he deepens the kiss. It's so intense he has to stabilize my back, so I don't topple over. The grasp of his hand on my neck and the warmth of his kiss erases the last vestiges of fear. This man is sturdy and strong. This is... right. This *fits.*

He can take me.

And damn, that's the sexiest part of it all. He's steady and strong, so damn *strong.*

We kiss until my lips feel bruised and swollen and still, it isn't enough. Moaning into his mouth, I squirm on his lap, loving the way his cock presses against my flaming hot ass. Tentatively, then with more conviction, I entwine my hands around his neck, allowing him to hold me but also claiming what's mine. The clean, woodsy smell of sandalwood and sheer unbridled masculinity, envelopes me, making me feel both powerful and feminine.

No one's ever kissed me like this, a kiss that needs no words, it's that demanding. Gently, he draws his hand from my neck and holds me, easing me onto the couch so that both of his knees are on either side of me, straddling me. He lowers himself to me. I moan, rising to meet him, needing more, deeper, *harder.* I gasp as one hand smoothes over my breasts until he finds my nipple, his thumb caressing over the hardened bud through the fabric of my clothing.

When his mouth leaves mine for a brief moment, I mewl involuntarily in protest. "I haven't made love in so damn long, Tobias," I whisper, a lone tear rolling down my cheek which he swipes away.

"Baby," he growls in my ear, a tortured plea not to tempt him, but I have to tell him.

"Ex-husband had a girl on the side, never slept with me. I figured he was making friends with his hand in the shower." He growls, taking my ear lobe between his teeth. I close my eyes and forge on. "Didn't know he was cheating on me. Last guy… my boyfriend… the one who was supposed to have his car keyed." His hands wrap around my waist, holding me close, as a warm, whiskery kiss trails along my jaw, then my collarbone, and lower still to the swell of my breasts. "I thought he was maybe gay," I say, my throat feeling tight but my body pulsing at his ministrations. "He never wanted to go all the way. I threw myself at him so hard I felt like a whore, and he said that relationships should transcend sex." I close my eyes as the flutter of kisses dip lower still, to my abdomen. "Oh, Tobias. Not there. My belly... it's so flabby."

A sharp smack hits my thigh, and I gasp.

"Rule number one," he says, his mouth hovering over my belly. "You do not make self-deprecating remarks. I won't allow it."

I'm not quite sure how I feel about that, but with my ass on fire and the lingering feel of his smack on my leg, I won't push it, not now.

"Your exes were assholes," he says with conviction. "Fucking morons. The man you're with ought to worship the ground you walk on."

"You're crazy," I whisper, though I can't hide the immense pleasure that courses through me at his words.

"I'm not the one who's crazy." He kisses lower, until the heat of his mouth hovers just above my pussy and *damn,* I'm turned on again, that quick. "You need to be more than fucked, Diana. Fucking is good in its own right," he says with a twitch of his lips. "And I'd be lying if I said I haven't fantasized about doing exactly that since the moment I laid eyes on you."

"Even when you were pissed?"

"Especially when I was pissed."

I giggle, then moan as his mouth returns to my fully-clothed body. He continues the trail of kisses to the top of my thighs, first the left, and then the right. Soft, fluttering warm, possessive touches of his mouth. My hips buck with a swipe of his tongue to my inner thigh. "Fuck me," he groans. "I can taste your honey even here. Jesus, baby, you're so ripe. I want to eat you out."

"Oh *God.*" I tremble. "I feel like a total slut, but I gotta admit there isn't a lot I'd say no to right now."

His low, deep chuckle makes my nipples harden. "You can be my slut," he says conversationally. "Deal?"

I grin as he swipes his tongue along my leg once more. "Yeeesssss." My voice breaks as I beg. "Please, Tobias. Please...sir."

He pushes himself up to his forearms, his dark eyes serious and stern, all traces of humor now gone. "Wanna make love to you, baby. I've been ready since the moment I caught you next to my car and I dreamed about taking you across my lap. Been imagining it ever since. You ready for that step?"

I nod. "I'm on the pill," I whisper.

"And I've got protection. Let's go to the bed."

He gets off the couch and takes me by the hand. I stand, stepping out of my shoes, both excited and nervous, but determined not to falter. I won't lose it now. I can't overthink this, or try to control this like I try to control every single goddamned thing in my life. And yet…

"I—I'm a control freak, Tobias."

He grins and gives me a playful smack. "You *were* a control freak. Also, not allowed with me."

I could seriously cry, his words bring such a relief to me, but the swat reignites the heat between my legs.

Okay. Alright. Okay. I can do this.

He gets up and leads me to the bed. "Let me undress you."

Not trusting my voice, I can only nod. But when he grasps the zipper and begins to draw it down, sending a shiver down my spine, a buzz sounds behind me. I freeze. The buzz sounds again, more insistent this time, and he looks to my bag.

"You need to get that?"

I groan. "It's my son. I'm so sorry. Everyone else is silenced but that's his call."

"Alright, babe. No worries. Go get it." He releases me, and I walk to the phone, cursing the timing. Chad is supposed to be with his father, he should be dealing with any issues.

"Diana, it's alright," Tobias assures me, likely picking up on my frustration. "I'm not goin' anywhere, honey." God, I love that he understands my son comes first.

Something in my chest dissolves, and I swallow hard, nodding, as I answer my phone.

"Hello?"

"Mom." Chad's sobs make my body go rigid. "Come get me. Please."

CHAPTER 10

I WATCH as her face goes from annoyed to wan, and she clasps one hand on her arm across her chest, as if to ward herself from whatever comes at her. "Chad, what is it, honey? What's going on? Where's your father?"

Her voice is laced with concern. Though I can't deny I feel chagrined that our plans are thwarted, I know her son comes first. I can feel the tension from where I sit, so I wait quietly. Patience and fortitude during intense times is something I've learned. First as an older brother, having to step into the role of man of the house at a young age, then later as a dominant.

"Chad, relax," Diana instructs in an even tone, her jaw tight, knuckles white from grasping the phone so hard. "Okay, honey. Remember how we talked about deep breathing? Take a deep breath in through your nose and exhale through your mouth. Good. Just like that. No, Chad, don't—" She sighs, and then she speaks again. "I can't get you right now, honey. It's your weekend with your dad, and he is supposed to be watching you." She swings her head around and her eyes meet mine, saddened, pleading even. I get to my feet, prepared to give her whatever she needs.

Her eyes briefly close before they flutter open again. "Put your father on the phone." Her lips thin, and when she opens her eyes again she's focused somewhere behind me as she listens. Her tone changes. "What did you show him?" she asks through gritted teeth, then listens. "*What?* Are you out of your mind? He'll have nightmares for weeks, thanks to you!" The voice on the other end of the phone grows louder, and my hands clench into fists as I watch her look change from horror-stricken, to angry, before she pales. "Come get him? *Now?* You *what?*"

I reach her and put a hand on her elbow. She jumps as if she just remembered that I'm in the room. "Just a minute," she says into the phone, taking it off her ear and tapping the mute button. When she looks at me, her eyes are filled with tears.

"What is it?"

"Billy, Chad's father, showed Chad a rated R *horror* film," she says, swiping her hand over her eyes. Her voice shakes when she speaks. Fuck, what I wouldn't give to make those eyes warm again, to calm the tremble in her voice. "He can handle some stuff, but horror… freaks him out. Badly."

"Jesus."

"Might seem like nothing, and a lot of eight-year-olds could handle it, I guess, I don't know, but Chad has nightmares and this particular one sent him over the edge." She waves the phone. "He called me in hysterics, wants me to pick him up. Billy says he needs to grow up and that I pamper him."

"Sounds like Billy's the one who needs to grow the fuck up."

Her eyes softened and she whispers, "Yeah. Chad wants to come home, but he asks me every week." She swallows, takes a deep breath, and carries on. "And Billy doesn't let him. Says it's time to cut the apron strings. But Billy just told me he wants him home, is dropping him off now." Her face falls. "Says he doesn't want his pussy for a son around him, and yeah, he said that in front of Chad. I'm so sorry. I need to go."

Christ.

I nod. "End the call, honey. I'll take you home."

She bites her lip, then put the phone back to her ear. "Hello? I'll be home in ten minutes. Put Chad on the phone." A pause, and then her voice softens. "Baby, you're coming home. It's going to be okay. It was just a movie, Chad." She nods. "See you soon. I love you."

She hangs up the phone. "He never says 'I love you' back," she says, and as soon as she's spoken, her cheeks flush. "I'm sorry. That just slipped out. It just—sometimes I need to hear it is all. I—I can't believe we were just about to—and then this happened." Her chin wavers, as she turns and faces the loveseat, clumsily lifting her shoes and sliding them on her feet.

I cross the room to her, needing to reassure her. What I wouldn't give to take this off her shoulders. In one swift motion, I pull her onto my lap. "C'mere," I say in a husky whisper. I pull her body into mine, and my arms encircle her. "I wanna tell you something. Not goin' anywhere, babe. Tonight was special, and you gave that to me. Your debt's wiped clean, and you and I, we move on from this. Tonight isn't our only chance. Okay?"

She nods. "Okay," she whispers. "Thank you for understanding."

"You're a brave girl, you know," I whisper back. "Now let's get you home and see to Chad, okay?"

She nods, but as I gently push her to her feet, she turns back to me, leans in, and brushes her lips across my cheek. I smile at her tender touch. No matter what it takes, I'll make her mine. If I have to wait. Fight for it. Slay her dragons. Whatever it takes, I'll make it happen. Something in me says *she's worth it.*

I lift her coat for her, helping her slide into it, then I pull it tight and zip it up.

"I can zip my own coat," she says, but when I lift a brow to her she smiles. "But thank you."

"Sounds to me like you take care of a lot of people in your life," I say. "Is that true?" I walk her to the door and open it for her.

"Yeah," she says. "Always been the way. I didn't have any brothers or sisters, but mom worked her fingers off. You know. So I did dinner after homework, stuff like that. My mom's older now, but independent. Chad's my only kid, but clearly, he needs me a little more than the average child. Hell, even the guys I've dated have always needed me." She laughs mirthlessly as we walk down the hall that leads to the back entrance, and the parking lot. The alternate exit allows us to skip walking past the crowded rooms in the main area of the club.

"Where are we going? And why does it smell like tobacco down here? You know, I really can help you with your décor."

"Different exit." I open the back door to Verge, revealing the well-lit back parking lot that all guests can access, though only employees usually do. "Smells like tobacco here because the club shares space with a smoke shop." I smile. "And we'll talk about décor."

"Ah, ok. You smoke?"

"Not anymore. Had a wild hair out of college, but I've tamed things down."

"Suuuure."

I give her a playful smack on the ass before I lead her to

the street. "So you're an interior decorator. Did I tell you what *I* do for work?"

Rubbing her ass, her cheeks are pink and eyes wide, she slides into the passenger seat. "No. I thought you owned this club?"

"Yep. I spank asses for a living."

She grins. "Hope it pays well."

I smirk and shut the passenger door, turning to the back lot and giving it a quick scan as I always do. Nothing out of place, nothing concerning. I glance at my phone, no messages.

"To your place, right?"

"Yes, please." We drive in comfortable silence for a few minutes before she speaks up. "What did you do before you owned Verge?"

"Lots of things. I mostly tended bar through college, then afterward made a good living as a bouncer."

"*Really.* Like one of those burly men at the door. That was you?"

I smirk. "Yeah, babe. I got offered a position as a personal bodyguard to a few semi-famous celebrities. Made good money doing that but the travel was killer. So I came back to bouncing here in NYC, and it made good money. I found a job as a bouncer for a BDSM club about ten years ago and things started to unfold then."

"Interesting. And that's how you met Seth?"

"Yep. Seth's wife, Rochelle, relocated here, got a job, the two of them were club regulars back in the day. Seth and I got tight, realized that we wanted more than a playground on someone else's turf. Launched Verge, and the rest is history."

"That's really cool."

"Glad you think so. I still keep it from my mama. I could be bodyguard to Prince for all she knows."

"Prince died like years ago."

My lips twitch. "We've tried telling her that maybe a dozen times. I don't lie to her. I just don't try to talk her out of what she knows."

Pretty, musical laughter fills the car, making me smile.

I easily navigate my car through the congested streets.

Her laughter dies, and her voice is softer now. I gently grasp her knee.

"Gonna be okay, Diana."

She puts her hand atop mine. "Thank you."

When we pull up to the curb, I hear a crashing sound, and it takes me a moment to realize it's the door slamming to a nondescript black car that Chad gets out of. I move quickly to open Diana's door, give Chad a quick wave, then step to the side as the boy practically tackles his mom. His little shoulders shake, and I realize he's crying. "Dad says if I'm too much of a wuss to handle a movie, he doesn't want me over anymore."

What a douchebag.

Diana holds her son, her eyes flashing toward the car Chad emerged from, and I feel my body go still.

I watch as a tall, very good-looking guy with longish light brown hair like Chad's comes over. He wears no coat in the frigid temps, just a hooded black sweatshirt and a pair of faded, dingy jeans. He stalks over to us, flicking his gaze to me, raking his eyes over me with undisguised scorn.

"Diana," he greets. "See you've got yourself another man of the hour."

My fists clench, but I hold my ground and stand back. This is her deal. If she needs me, I'll wade in. Hell, I'm already yearning to bust this guy's jaw, but I won't do anyone favors by escalating shit. Instead, I look to Chad and shoot him a smile.

"Chad, what's up, man?" I reach to Chad to greet him with

a fist bump. At first Chad just stares, then tentatively makes a fist of his own and gently smacks my knuckles.

"Hi," Chad says. "You're the guy from the bakery."

I nod. "Yup."

"Talked me into eating the other donut."

"That I did."

"Billy, meet Tobias," Diana says. "Tobias, Billy, Chad's father."

Billy looks at my outstretched hand and shoves his own in his pocket. "I'm more than Chad's father," Billy says, his lip curled. "I'm Diana's husband."

Diana exhales angrily and my body goes still. Her *husband?* Have I been played?

"My *ex*-husband," she hisses. "You have no right to call yourself that anymore. But I'm not wasting any more time on *that* conversation. Why'd you take him to that movie?"

I narrow my eyes back on Billy. Fucking jerk, pretending he has a claim to her he'd already wasted.

Billy purses his lips and rolls his eyes. "That matters?"

"Yes," Diana says, while I mentally recite the alphabet in German. I don't wanna lose my temper.

"*Apocalypse Dawn* is the tamest horror film in a decade and he lost it."

"He's *eight,*" Diana says through gritted teeth.

"Yeah? He would be if you let him grow the fuck up. Acts like he's six. Not sure why you get your rocks off keeping him young, but whatever works for you, babe."

The boy buries his head on his mother's shoulder.

A gust of wind blows hard, making both Diana and Chad shiver. I've had enough.

"Pleased to meet you," I lie, facing Billy. "Diana, why don't you take Chad out of the cold now."

Diana looks at me and nods. "We'll talk tomorrow, Billy," she says, turning her back on him.

"So that's how it goes now?" Billy says. "You put out for some big, burly guy and he comes and bosses everyone, including you, around?"

"Ignore him, Diana, and go in the house," I instruct quietly. "Chad's freezing, and this guy's only baiting you." I turn my full attention on her, making sure she listens, but more importantly, making sure she stays safe. She nods, ushering Chad toward her front door. When they're gone, I turn to Billy. I imagine the satisfying crunch of the asshole's jaw snapping back as I deck him, those arrogant eyes no longer focused on Diana, his words no longer injuring the boy who shakes in his mother's arms.

The guy has to be either drunk or off his nut, since he merely glares back. "And you, time for you to get your ass in your car, and get the hell out of here," I tell him, my voice brooking no argument. I'm so done with this asshole. Billy only glares. "Unless," I say patiently, "You need a little help in that department? Need an escort?" I loosen my shoulders and crack my neck, then take a step toward him. *Please, asshole, give me a reason to hurt you.*

"You put your hands on me, I call the police," Billy threatens.

I laugh out loud. "Please do. Ask for officer Zack Williams. He's one of my closest friends, and he'd be happy to come here and help avoid a domestic disturbance this fine evening."

Billy's eyes narrow. "Fuck you," he hisses, but he moves toward his car despite his apparent bravery, and when he slams the door shut, I hear the click of a lock.

Motherfucker. I can feel the adrenaline heating my gut, the surge of power that shoots through me. The nerve of the asshole treating not only Diana but her son like shit. He needs a goddamned lesson, and I want to be the one to give it to him. I won't stoop to his level, though.

I stand, arms crossed on my chest, oblivious to the biting wind that nips at me. I watch until Billy pulls away from the curb and his taillights are no longer visible, before I turn and go to Diana.

"I've never seen him do that before," Diana whispers over the sleeping head of her son.

"What's that?"

"Hold someone's hand other than mine before he goes to sleep, and do it so… relaxed." She reaches over and tucks a stray strand of hair behind Chad's ear, frowning.

As an older brother to three younger siblings, when my dad took off I took on a role that veered into paternal. I'd done it all, taking on the fatherly role they all needed—baseball practice, putting kids to bed, setting rules and discipline in place. My youngest sister had only been two when my dad left, and my mom worked the overnight shift because it brought in extra income. I'd scared the boogey monster out of my baby sister's closet, read her bedtime stories, and given her the reassurance she needed to rest well. Even though she's a busy college student now, she calls me once a week, and we're still tight. I still remember her as the little girl who called me Toby, the only one who ever had.

"Billy's an asshole," she continues. "And if I didn't have to honor the court-ordered visitation rights, I wouldn't do it. I know kids need moms and dads. I mean, I guess it's best for them. I know Billy's his father, and Billy has the right to see him." She bites her lip. "I've seen families torn apart by divorce, and I fought it, Tobias. I wanted it to work. I didn't want to be one of *those* families that split holidays. Billy just never understood Chad."

"Lots of people don't," I say gently, taking the hand that

rests on her sleeping child in mine. "Not saying it's right, and you didn't need to tell me Billy's an asshole. Knew it from the minute he opened his mouth. And yeah, I agree with you that kids should see their dads, and that dads have the right to see their kids."

"Doesn't mean it's easy," she whispers.

"No."

She swallows before speaking again. "Every time he sees him, we regress a little. For a long time, I thought it was because visiting Billy reminded him of what we once had, and I blamed myself for the regression."

"Baby..."

"But it isn't that," she interrupts. "No. I know now, it's not me. It's Billy. *He* does this to him. He wants Chad to be that strong, macho boy *he* was. And Chad isn't that kid."

I know she needs me to listen, but it's more than that. I want to know who she is. What makes her tick. Listening to her clues me in.

"He... he would crumple in a football game. He doesn't even like high fives, never has. They startle him and he says it hurts." She smiles sadly, but her eyes are bright. "That's why he liked the fist bump thing you did. It doesn't scare him. He talked about it all day long."

My gut clenches at that, but I only nod and give her an encouraging smile.

"He doesn't like when the seams on his socks cross his foot." She seems embarrassed after she states the seemingly random fact.

I shrug. "I don't like that either."

She laughs softly, then stops when Chad stirs. "Billy made him wear the seams crooked for days, said getting used to discomfort was part of learning to be a man."

"Jesus."

"And yeah, I get it. Chad *does* need to learn things, and

maybe I'm too lenient on him. But he's sensitive, and I have a whole team of people I work with. He's made huge progress. The very fact he let you touch him..." her voice wavers a bit and she ends with a whisper. "You have no idea."

She smoothes down her son's hair and smiles. "You've done enough, Tobias. Why don't you go home? I'm so sorry our night ended so abruptly."

I shake my head. "I'm gonna stay as long as you need me. Got no plans. Checked in at Verge, no one needs me, and all's quiet with Zack."

She nods, biting her lip and looks out the window before she asks, "So what's the deal with the attacks? Any more word?"

I shake my head. "First victim said she met him outside of Verge, NYPD assumed he'd come from there. Evidence seemed to point to him being a member, but the investigation got us nowhere." I pause. "Second victim didn't survive, so we've got nothing, except that her body was found not too far away."

"My God."

"Yeah. We haven't had a serial rapist around here in a good long time. Random acts of violence, crime, hell yeah. But a serial attacker? Not that I remember. But no. No more news tonight and we don't need to talk about that before you go to bed." I sober. I don't want to give her anything to fear, but I also need her to be safe. "I want you to listen. This guy is still at large. You *have* to be careful, Diana. You understand? I wanna see you again, and I want you listening to every instruction I give you without question."

She swallows and nods, her eyes bright. "You want to see me again?"

My grip on her hand tightens. See her again? Hell, I don't want to leave. "Absolutely."

She bites her lip and looks at me coyly. "You know what

sucks? I've been absolutely *dying* to have a good spanking followed by hot as Hades sex, and we got cut short."

I quietly laugh. "That we did. How's that ass?"

She squirms. "Sore as hell."

Fuck. I need her alone.

"Can you put Chad to bed now?"

She grins. "Hell yeah."

CHAPTER 11

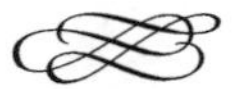

"LET me see that ass of yours," he orders. Tobias stands in nothing but boxers at the foot of my bed, and I'm on all fours, my knees and the palms of my hands braced on the comforter at the center of my bed. "Belly down, arch that back for me." He's commanding and it's so fucking delicious, my thighs are damp. He leans over, places his hand on the small of my back, and smacks my ass, hard. I lay my full weight on the bed as both of his hands go to my hips.

"Jesus, you're gorgeous," he growls, stepping closer to the bed and pushing his flank against the heat on my backside.

"Thanks," I murmur, eyes shut tight. "Just don't look at my belly."

He spanks me again, harder this time. "What'd I tell you about making comments about your body? You're beautiful, Diana, and I don't wanna hear anything else about that."

"It's your job to say that." I turn my head to the side, not looking at him.

"Diana," he says, his voice sharp. "I'm serious. You talk shit about your body, I'll take my belt to your ass."

That makes my heart thump. Not saying anything out

loud about my body will be hard, and I don't want to be punished, but hell, the idea of him taking off his belt makes me squirm.

He runs his hand over my soft, silky skin. "On your back, baby," he orders. I flip over eagerly. "Seen every inch of you, sweetheart," he says, straddling me with one knee on either side, and whispers. "Liked every inch of what I've seen. You hear me? Every. Fucking. *Inch.*"

I mewl as his hard cock presses up against my pussy.

"I'm not the kinda girl who sleeps with a guy one day after meeting him," I whisper, my voice oddly shaky. "I–I don't want you to get the wrong idea."

He chuckles. "Girl like you ought to take pleasure in a body like this. You told me you haven't been fucked in years. Baby, allow me the honor. I promise, I won't tell your mama."

I laugh out loud. "Don't talk about my mama with your cock pressed up against me," I plead. "Way to kill a mood."

He grins, while allowing me a moment to ogle him. His large, muscled frame makes me feel small and feminine, his shoulders dwarfing my own. "Dude, you're like… this muscle man. And I'm like…"

A low growl warns me. "Don't go there." I swallow and don't complete my thought. He's already spanked me and I'm not gonna push it.

"Not a muscle man. I like control, I like strength, I push my body to the extreme. Need to."

"Well if pushing your body to the extreme gives you *this,* then hell yeah, push away, honey."

He captures my wrists and pulls them above my head, smiling, his eyes heated. "Stay here," he says. "Don't move those arms, babe. I wanna fuck you and I wanna do it on my terms. I like control on a normal day. In bed? I like it *completely.*"

Yessss.

I swallow hard and nod. As he lowers his body down to mine, my breasts pushed up against him, my heart skips a crazy beat in my chest. He nudges his cock at my entrance, having already put a condom on before he joined me in bed.

"You ready?" he asks in a growl against the shell of my ear. I whimper in return, and the grip on my wrists tightens to almost painful, my heartbeat spikes. "Answer, baby."

"Yes," I gasp. "Yes, oh God, please, yes. I'm so ready."

He responds with a low growl, pushing his cock to my entrance and sliding against the slickness. "Oh, yeah," he groans. "So fucking wet. Wanna fuck this pussy." I whimper with need, opening my legs even wider, needing to send him the message that *yes,* fucking me good and hard is a good thing and he needs to hurry it up already.

"Tell me if you need me to slow down," he whispers in a low, raspy growl. "Haven't been fucked in a while, could overwhelm you. I'm in control in the bedroom but you give me the lead. Got it, baby?"

I nod. I like that. He wants to fuck me, on his terms and hard, but he won't take me beyond what I can handle.

With a gentle yet firm push, he slides inside, filling me. My head falls to the side and my eyelids flutter shut. "Yessss. Oh, God, *yes.*"

Holding my wrists tight, he pushes firmer lifting my hips and thrusting once more, amping up my arousal. My clit throbs and my pussy milks his cock. I need more, harder, faster.

"Yes," I breathe, and he responds with another hard thrust, the rhythm of pleasure ripping through every inch of me, my nerves on fire. His mouth slides to my neck, a swipe of his tongue makes me shiver, my hips buck as his teeth sink into the tender skin of my throat. He trails his tongue over the place he bit before pulling my flesh into his mouth with a firm suckle. It's so fucking hot my pelvis bucks beneath him, the pleasure-pain intense.

He moves his mouth to mine, then releases one wrist, weaving his fingers through my hair. He wraps it around his fingers and tugs, forcing my head back, a spike of fear and pleasure makes my need rise. He pushes hard then soft, releases my mouth, and brings his lips to my jaw, kissing as he makes his way down my neck once more. He's not just making love to me, he's worshiping me. I fucking love it.

"Tobias," I pant, my body hot and damp. Suddenly, he pulls out. Is he done? Fuck, no, he hasn't—

"On your knees. Wanna fuck that pussy from behind. Got a taste of that skin, need more."

His sharp command washes over me, and I scramble onto all fours, following his lead as a gentle shove of his hand makes my torso hit the bed before he grasps my hips from behind. He shoves his hardened cock between my folds.

"*Fuck,* yeah," he growls. "Yeah, that's what I like." He pounds into me, drawing my head back with a fist of hair at my nape.

"I'm gonna come," I breathe, unable to hold myself back, my pelvis jerking from every thrust of his cock, hips bucking as waves of pleasure build me up.

"Baby," he murmurs into my ear, his firm hold on my hips tightening. "Come for me. Let yourself go. Anytime you're ready."

I'm so ready. With a low sound half purr and growl, I fly over the edge of ecstasy. Light explodes behind my eyelids, a low, guttural groan washing over me, the fulfilling sound of his own climax making me grin with pleasure. He slows his thrusts and drops his head to my neck, his stubble scratching the sensitive skin. I needed this.

"*Christ.*" He lowers his torso onto my back, the two of us

sweaty and panting, reveling in the afterglow. "So fucking good."

"Mmm," is all I can manage, now that I'm ready to collapse from exhaustion.

"Gonna pull out, Diana. Need to clean you up and tuck you in."

Tuck me in? I watch him over my shoulder, wordlessly, as he slowly pulls out. I whimper at the loss. He lifts his boxers and tucks his cock back in, then pads to the bathroom. He comes back a moment later with a damp, warm washcloth. I'm still frozen on the bed, half drunk, ass in the air.

He gives my upturned backside a playful smack. "On your back, let me clean you now."

Without conscious thought, I obey, loving how nice it is to just listen and not think.

"Spread your legs."

Again, I obey.

The warm washcloth trails between my legs, followed by a soft towel. He tosses both into the hamper next to my closet, then slides into bed beside me.

"I should go," he murmurs, reluctantly. "If Chad wakes up and sees me here—"

At first, I hate the idea of him leaving after what we just shared, but I can't help but admire his motives. He doesn't want to mess my boy up.

"It's okay," I whisper. "My gut says he's out for the night and I'll shut the door so he has to knock. You're welcome to stay. Do you get up early?"

"Yeah."

"You can leave before he's even up. I'll get you breakfast or coffee or both, then see you off. Okay?"

He smiles. "Absolutely." I reluctantly get out of bed and pull on shorts and a tank.

"Gotta have something on case Chad needs me," I explain.

"Then I'll allow you to wear those for now." His lips twitch and he closes his eyes.

"Allow?"

He opens one eye and fixes me with a look. "Did you somehow forget that you just hooked up with a dom, honey? Didn't make that clear enough?"

I grin, sidling up to him in bed. I feel immediately at ease with him, and it surprises me. Here's a man who can be gentle and stern, funny and sweet, and though my mind warns me, *don't do it, don't fall for it, things are never as good as they seem,* I somehow can't help it.

"So under normal circumstances, no clothes to bed?"

"Of course not."

I bite my tongue. I almost make another comment about my body. I'm not sure I'm comfortable enough in my own skin to sleep naked, but saying so might get me spanked, so I need to play it safe.

"I want access to these curves whenever I want," he says, opening just one eye now. "And believe me, I'll make it worth your while, honey."

Though I've just come harder than I have in recent memory, maybe even *ever,* his words trip my heartbeat up once more, my pussy heating with desire. God, the man's addictive.

"Well maybe someday we can give that a shot. Tonight, I'm beat."

Beatrice would say I'm out of my mind, sharing my bed with this man. My mama would have stronger words, and I'm not even sure how I feel about it myself, but it feels so nice to be held by someone strong. Someone who knows how to treat me like a woman.

He lifts the covers and tucks them in around my shoulders and sides, making sudden tears spring to my eyes. I haven't been tucked in since I was a child, and even then, it was rare.

"Night, Tobias," I whisper into the dark.

"Night, Diana," he murmurs. Soon I feel his breathing slow, his body rising and falling as he sleeps. I stare into the darkness, wanting to hold onto this, to make the moment last forever, so that when it's gone I can conjure it up again and somehow recreate this feeling of comfort and peace. Sleeping alone will suck after this.

I try to stay awake but my eyelids flutter closed, the warm blankets and body beside me like a lullaby, easing me to sleep. And as slumber descends, one thought plagues me. I can't hold onto this moment. It isn't mine to keep.

I WAKE the next morning to the smell of coffee and a note resting up against my travel mug. It sits next to my bed. I pick up the note.

Had to go. I didn't want to wake you, you were sleeping so peacefully. Call me later?

My eyes still heavy with sleep, I rub the heels of my hands in them to wake up, yawn, and push myself to sitting, stretching my arms over my head. I don't like knowing he's gone and I missed saying good-bye. I pick up the mug, take a sip, and sigh. The coffee's still piping hot and exactly what I need. Clearly, he found my French Vanilla creamer, too. Okay, yeah, so that's sorta like a kiss.

I will not fall for him. I can't fall for him.

So desperate for companionship and validation, I married Billy after one amazing night at the Hard Rock Casino in Reno, and I came to regret it. I dated my last boyfriend only twice before I practically decided to marry him, *even though* the guy didn't sleep with me because, as I now know, he was getting some on the side. I made stupid, rash decisions and lived to regret them. *I would not do that again.*

As I shift on the bed, my ass aches with a soothing sort of burn that I can't begin to decipher. I bite my lip, tentatively touching the skin that's still hot. I'd been spanked by the Big Bad Dom, and that had only been the beginning. I can't wait to get Beatrice on the phone and tell her everything. I don't have to wait long. My phone buzzes.

How was it?!?!!? Was he amazing? Did he kiss you? Did you do a "scene" at the "CLUB?"

I snicker at her liberal use of punctuation.

Yes, yes, and yes, until Chad called me in hysterics because Billy took him to that zombie movie.

Her response is immediate. *OH MY GOD. I'LL KILL HIM WITH MY OWN BARE HANDS.*

Her protective attitude toward my son makes me smile. *Thanks, but it's okay now. Tobias came with me to deal with Billy.*

He didn't!

He did! I think he scared the shit out of Billy, too, which was worth the whole date right there.

Damn right. You sure you really got it for this guy? Cuz I might propose. Leave it to Beatrice to hit the nail on the head.

I smile and bite my lip, but before I can reply, another text comes in, this one from Tobias.

Good morning, sunshine.

Warmth floods through me at the greeting. *Morning, handsome.*

Something I want to ask you to do today, please.

Beatrice is still texting me like a madwoman. *Are you going to see him again today?*

I shake my head even though she can't see me. *I don't know.*

Excuse me?

I blink in confusion before I realize my "I don't know" meant for Beatrice actually went to Tobias. Shit!

Oh, sorry! Wrong text!

Beatrice is just gonna have to wait. I can't risk pissing off the dom with multi text conversations.

Diana, I'd like your undivided attention, please. I'll wait until you're ready.

I can *hear* the deep command through the text. And there it was again. He wants my attention, but he'll wait, instead of selfishly demanding it this instant.

Swallowing, already chastened, I respond. *Yes, sir.*

I have just one thing I'm going to ask you to do today, and then I'll let you get on with whatever else you need to do.

Yes. Got it.

Throughout the day, at least three times, I want you to text me something you like about yourself. I'd much prefer more than three, but three is a good start. Understood?

Is he serious? I stare at the phone, mouth agape for a moment, before I respond.

Yes, sir. I understand. Will do.

Any less than that, and our next meeting will begin with you over my knee.

Well, shit. Now he's getting me worked up again.

Yes, sir.

Good girl. Start now, please, before I have to go and you do, too.

Blinking, I stroke my chin. I hear Chad stirring in the other room. Once he comes in, depending on his mood, my focus will be way off.

Okay, alright. Hmmmm...

I make really kickass pancakes.

Beatrice's text comes in as I hit send.

Helloooo? Yoohooo? Did you get kidnapped by aliens with twitchy palms?

Tobias' response comes in next. *Very good. I love pancakes, especially with butter and real maple syrup. Make me some sometime?*

My stomach churns with hunger.

Yes, absolutely, sir.

That's good for now. I look forward to your texts later. xx

I blink at the little x's on the bottom of the screen. He blew me a kiss! Or… something. Do text x's count? Still, it's promising.

"Mom!" Chad bangs on the door seconds before he pushes it in and enters. My phone buzzes with another text.

Hi. My name is Beatrice. Not sure you remember me from way back when, but we used to be best friends sharing juicy deets of a first date, and now I'm dying from lack of attention and needing to supply my own juicy details which I assure you, are not as good as the real deal and maybe would even get me checked into a psych unit or maybe jail.

I snicker. Brat.

Hey. Tobias was texting me, and doms don't wait. So apparently you must be a domme or something.

This comes as a surprise to you?

I shake my head and pat the bed for Chad to join me. He sits on the edge primly, already dressed for the day.

"I'm texting your Aunt Bea, who's being a bit impatient."

"Oh okay. Did the man go? I hoped he'd be here when I woke up."

He did?

"Really?"

"Yes. I like him, a lot, and thought maybe if he was here he'd buy us donuts again." I laugh and ruffle his hair, which makes him pull away but smile.

"Maybe he will," I say. "But not today. I'll see if we can see him again."

And somehow, right then, knowing my boy likes him, my affection for Tobias grows.

Damn.

But I have to be careful. What if he isn't the kind of guy I want around my son? What if he isn't dependable? What if…?

I close my eyes briefly and take in a deep breath. I'm falling for him, hard, and need to make sure I don't hurt myself, or, worse, Chad along the way.

CHAPTER 12

I FILE the bills I paid, and update the spreadsheet I share with Seth. It's been two days since I've seen Diana, and miss her, the need to see her again a distraction. Seth sits across from me, sipping his coffee, looking over the monthly bookkeeping. He wads up the paper from our late afternoon lunch, and tosses it into the barrel by my desk.

"Looks good," Seth says. "Turning quite a profit already, much more so than the average start-up business."

"Yeah," I agree. "Things are lookin' good, man."

Seth puts the sheets onto the table and sits back in his chair, fixing me with a stare. "How are things looking with you and Diana?"

"Fine," I answer noncommittally, not quite ready to get into it with Seth yet.

Seth takes another sip of coffee. "She familiar with the scene?"

"Not at all."

"Even better."

I think for a moment, eyeing Seth. "Yeah?"

He nods. "Could be helpful. Girls who are familiar with

the scene don't give you shit for basic expectations and don't freak out as easily. Typically, won't run if you go caveman on them, and is ready to stand some pain. But, that always comes with baggage from a previous dom's training."

I nod.

"Girl new to the scene, you get to break her in."

I snort. "You talk about it like she's a horse or something."

He grins. "You know I treat Rochelle like a princess. Love the ground she fuckin' walks on. So you can call my talk whatever the hell you want, doesn't change who I am or how I behave. You know what I mean."

Seth and I don't have personal talks like this much, mostly minding our own business. I'm experienced enough to know Seth has a point. Still, I'm ready to change the subject.

"You hear anything from Zack?"

Seth frowns. "No. Seems our perp's gone dark. Son of a bitch. Wish I could catch him myself."

"Same."

"Seems to me the quiet isn't a good thing. Like the calm before the storm, you know?"

"Exactly." I look to the right, where one lone window stands in the otherwise dark office. Outside my window, pedestrians walk by, bundled in scarves and winter coats. The biting winter wind hasn't lessened with impending snow in the forecast. Is one of the people who walks by my window the man who hurt those women? Is one of those women a future target? Zack's team made it clear. The perpetrator has a motive, and he has a pattern.

"Maybe time to get an undercover agent here?" I ask. "Have Zack find someone on the force willing to play a dom for a while?"

Seth shakes his head. "I don't like that idea. Doesn't seem

right to take advantage of subs who think they're here to scene."

"No, you don't understand," I explain. "Not my point. Find an officer who *is* a dom to play in scenes. Get a good read on the others here playing."

Seth shrugs a shoulder. "The integrity of this club is at stake if we fuck around with memberships and shit like that."

"Lives of the members are at stake if we don't," I counter. We battle silently with stares for a moment.

"Zack's already a member here. He hasn't scened in a while, but we can invite him to. Get him right here in on the action," Seth says.

"Yeah. I like that."

Seth nods. "You'd suggested anyone else, not sure I'd agree. Trust Zack with my life."

"Let's see how this plays out. Instinct could be wrong, but I wouldn't bet on it."

"Agreed."

My phone buzzes and I pick it up without thinking.

I've got really, really great boobs. Tits. Breasts. Whatever you wanna call them.

My dick hardens and I shift on my seat, biting back a grin before I respond.

Good girl and yes, you do.

I've kept up making her text me something nice about herself.

A low whistle gets my attention. Seth's grinning at me.

"Known you for ten years," Seth says. "And that's the first time I've ever seen you lose your concentration over a *text*. You're just not that guy." His shoulders shake. "Diana?"

"Shut it."

"Nope. You razzed the shit outta me with Rochelle, and, you know, karma and all that. You just totally went AWOL on me and grinned like a guy who won the lottery, looking at your phone." He shakes his head. "Gonna tell Rochelle to start writing up the wedding invitation list."

I wanna deck the grin right off his face, but I know the code of the brotherhood: you love a guy like a brother, you give him shit about a serious girl. If Seth didn't like Diana, or thought it was no more than a one-night stand, he wouldn't bother.

"For real, man, you want to come to our place for dinner? Bring Diana?"

"Not sure. She's got a kid, and he's got special needs."

Seth's brows shoot up. "No shit."

"No shit."

He nods silently, then says, "Open invitation, man. *Mi casa es su casa* and all that shit." He stands. "Let me know if you hear from Zack again, and I'll see you tonight?"

"Later."

I ignore my phone until Seth leaves.

I can be a very good listener. I'm patient and attentive, and don't interrupt or try to solve things. I just... listen when I need to. Which, when your best friend is Beatrice, is often.

I grin.

I like that. Good girl. You've given me your five. Tomorrow, you'll be required to do six.

A beat passes before she responds, then, *Yes, sir. But soon, I'll run out of things, you know.*

I smile, my chest warming and tightening with something inexplicable. *At that point, I'll help you.*

Thank you.

Of course. Hey, they have the skating in the park this week. Supposed to be chilly but bearable tonight. Can I take you?

Her response is quick and disappointing. *Chad won't skate. :(*

Ah. Life is complicated dating a woman with a kid, but this is what I'm getting into.

My mind goes back to the morning I woke up next to her, when I pushed myself with reluctance out of her bed. Seeing her lying curled up next to me, her wild mane of crazy curls askew on the pillow, her creamy skin soft and relaxed, something primal in me stirred to life.

Mine.

I'd tucked the blanket back in around her, scrawled her a note, and peeked in on the sleeping boy. Before I left, I made her a cup of coffee and found a thermos that would keep it hot, then left it for her to find on her nightstand. I want this. All of it. Not just the sex or the kink but the companionship. The warmth of family, comfort of home, and a woman who can take on a man like me.

As we text, building an easy camaraderie, I realize I have decisions to make. I don't act on impulse, or make rash decisions, but think things through with precision, and one thing's clear: my relationship with Diana will always be impacted by the fact that she has a child. If we're a thing, I accept that.

I send her a response. *Maybe some other time. I suck at skating anyway, just thought it'd be romantic and shit. Next week they're having the NYC kids' movie festival?*

Just me and you?

Could Chad handle it? I ask.

I think so. Depends on what they're showing and how much I can bribe him with popcorn and gummy bears.

I grin to myself. *Want me to ask him?*

I'd like that. You're amazing, you know that? <3

I shake my head. Her simple appreciation makes me smile. It's amazing that I want to take a woman and her son to a movie festival? Hardly. Doctors who perform open heart surgery, that's amazing. People who adopt sick kids from third world countries? Also, amazing. That guy I'd seen in Central Park painting murals of the Seven Wonders of the

World with his bare hands, then donating the proceeds of his sales to charity? Also *amazing.*

Seems Diana hasn't had much "normal nice guy" in her life.

Not sure about that, but thanks, babe. Opening our doors shortly to the evening crowd, and I'm on for Dungeon Monitor tonight.

Okay so that sounds ridiculously sexy.

I smile. *Need to get you here and see for yourself.*

Her response heats my blood. *Yes, please!*

You free tonight?

Unfortunately, not. :(

Ok well be a good girl, and we'll make plans soon.

Yes, sir. Have fun.

I put my phone back on my desk, my mind a swirl of questions with few answers, but one thing I know for sure: the next time she comes here, I'll make sure she enjoys the hell out of it.

A knock sounds on the doorframe to my office, and I look up. I rarely shut my door, but still prefer people knock before entering. Travis enters,

"Hey, you hear anything from the boys next door lately? Brax went out for a smoke break, came back, says there was a scuffle out back."

"Nothin'. Like to think they mind their business, we mind ours. They seem like a few hotheads, if you ask me, but I stay out of it."

"Alright," Travis pushes to his feet. "Just wonderin'. How's Diana?"

I feel my jaw tighten. Do I live in a fucking fish bowl?

"She's good. Can't come tonight, no babysitter on Sunday nights."

"My girlfriend's kid sister babysits," he says. "High school senior, always looking for more hours. Want me to give you her number?"

I shake my head. "Nah. I'll ask her when I see her, but I think she's picky about who watches Chad." Travis nods. "Her son has special needs. That doesn't leave this office, though, okay? Not sure she wants everyone knowin' her shit."

"Course. What kinda special needs?"

"Looks like spectrum, but high functioning. Maybe OCD."

Travis nods. "Kid sister's the same," he says. "Takes a lotta patience and time to parent one of those kids. Swear to God my mama was gray at thirty."

"That's your doin', not your sister's."

Travis grins. "Likely."

"Alright, gonna prep stuff at the bar."

"Good luck. I'll come in with you in a few and give you a hand."

Another knock sounds on the doorframe, and we both look. Brax stands with a large box in hand. "UPS delivery. Who ordered the My Little Pony Dreamhouse?"

"It's the *Barbie* Dreamhouse, dumbass," Travis says, shaking his head with an eye roll. "My Little Pony has the Crystal Castle."

"And you know this how, *princess*?" Brax jabs good-naturedly.

"He's got sisters, Brax, lay off. Give me the box, man."

Brax hands it to me, and I pull a blade out of my back pocket, slipping it through the packing tape. I smile, the scent of leather filling my nostrils. "Oh, yeah. Took some time, but they're finally here."

I pull four thick leather bags out of the box and lay them on my desk, then pull the drawstring to one. I lay out a dozen soft black floggers with hand-cut handles, a variety of different fraternity paddles of all shapes and sizes, and half a dozen solid-looking leather straps, among other things.

"Fuck me," Brax mutters, picking up one of the straps. "This is high quality shit. You've got enough to start a small school for BDSM 101." He picks up one of the heavier paddles and swings it against his palm, then flinches. "Ok so maybe intermediate school. Who's on Dungeon duty tonight?"

"That'd be me," I say, snatching the paddle away from Brax. "Some of these don't go on the floor unless they're tested," he said, "but some will be for re-sale on a party night."

"When's the next party?"

"Not for a while. Seth and I aren't down with inviting party guests until this assault shit has been put behind us."

"Fair enough," Brax says.

They sit in reverent silence as I stand, testing each implement out on my hand. "Yeah, these are good quality. Zack's friend on the West Coast supplies him and hooked me up, gave me a bulk rate."

"Only you'd get a bulk rate on frat paddles," Travis says, shaking his head with a grin. "See y'all later."

I leave one bag out and put the rest away.

"Tough job, checking quality control," Brax says with mock seriousness. "You got one or two you don't wanna do, let me know. I'd be willing to help a brother out."

"Might take you up on that. Not sure I want to test these out on a sub yet. You wanna bottom for me and let me know what you think? Got a hidden switch in there?"

Brax punches my shoulder. "Fuck you."

I grin at him. "Thanks, man." Deep down, I know there's only one submissive whose ass I want to paint with my new toys, and she isn't here tonight.

I walk past the lobby to the bar area. Guests have begun to arrive, many greeting me but keeping their distance, several eyeing the trademark leather bag in my hand. I walk past the bar and dungeon and head to the party room. When things settle down, we'll schedule another high protocol party, one of the most profitable options we offer at Verge. We host babygirls and their daddies, masters and slaves, some 24/7 couples, and others who just hook up for the night. It's fun and sexy, and the parties are renowned up and down the East Coast.

Brax follows me as I inspect the tables, chairs, and accoutrements we use for our parties. "Gotta book some more parties. They earned over sixty percent of our profit last year. Seth says he wants more, but he's so busy these days." He still travels on weekends to Boston to work with his friend and former employer at Limits, the club where he'd gotten his start. The owner of Limits and his wife just welcomed another child, and Seth needs to oversee things there as well.

"Need a damn secretary," I mutter.

"Don't disagree," Brax replies. "This has gotten bigger than either of you ever planned, huh?"

"Fuck yeah."

We leave the party room and head back to the dungeon. I want to find someone willing to test out implements and I know as the night wears on, it'll get more crowded in here. As I turn the corner, Axle walks by, his short graying hair spiky, blue eyes keenly eyeing the bag in my hand. Marla, regular member and the owner of a local bookstore, follows. She's a petite woman with short black hair and a cute pair of glasses perched on her nose.

"Mmm. Got some new toys there, boss?" Axle asks. Marla's eyes grow curious.

"Yep. New shipment that needs to be tested. I need someone who's willing to give these a shot and rate them for quality."

Axle grins. "I'd be game." He pauses, seeing the wicked gleam in Brax's eye and quickly amends, "as *top,* asshole, so don't get any ideas."

Marla eyes them with interest. "You need a sub for a demo?"

"Not really a demo, more like a test run."

"Totally game here." She stands with her hands on her hips, wearing a tight-fitting black tank top and black leggings that are practically painted on. "I've had one helluva week. So stressful, you have no idea. Would give anything for a really, *really* good spanking. Just sayin'."

I hand the bag to Axle. "You know the routine. Get—"

"Yeah, yeah, c'mon, boss, I look like a newbie?" Axle grits out. "I've spanked Marla's ass more times than I've kissed my own mother. We know each other well, don't we, kiddo?"

Marla's eyes flash at him. Apparently, not well enough to know that "kiddo" grates on her. "Yep," she says. "And Master Axle can take me to where I need to go. He knows my hard limits, knows what I like and what I don't."

"Good deal. Have fun."

Brax stays behind as I take my leave, nearly crashing into a petite woman who's on her way in. "Oh. Hello, Master Tobias." Her voice is high and breathy when she speaks. She casts her eyes down, her voice demure. She knows me, but do I know her? As owner of the club, people often recognize me before I do them. She has chin-length blonde hair, a small, rounded face with a pointed nose. She's wearing bright red lipstick and stark black eye make-up. She has bright, vivid silver and red earrings with a matching choker. I do a double take. No, she isn't wearing a choker. It's *tattooed* on.

"Hi," I say. "Excuse me."

"Sir?" Her question stops me as I make my way to the exit. Though it's common, even expected, for a submissive to refer to me as *sir,* it grates on me now. I only want to hear Diana say it.

"Yes?" I turn back to the woman, trying hard to stay patient. It's not her fault I'm on edge and want Diana here instead of her.

"Are you…" her voice trails off and she bites her lip. "Are you on for Dungeon Monitor tonight, sir?"

"I am."

"Will you be… needing anyone for a demonstration? Or… perhaps in need of, um…" it seems her bravado fails her as she doesn't complete her sentence.

"I'm sorry," I respond. "I'm not going to scene with anyone tonight, if that's what you're asking."

"Oh," she says, her face falling. Normally, I'd leap at the chance of a demonstration, especially on a night when I really need some good stress relief. I love topping, crave the control and power like a drug. But no. Even though I've only just met Diana, it feels like cheating to scene with another woman. Scening *can* be detached but there's a certain intimacy to it, I can't bring myself to share that with anyone else.

"But there's no shortage of doms here. I'm happy to help you find one?"

She nods, her eyes now eager. "Please, sir. I've been watching for weeks now, and I'm finally ready to try it. I wanted to ask an experienced dom who knows how to take it easy on me."

Right, then. Too bad Travis is occupied. The man has a gentle touch unlike many other doms who grace the doors of Verge. Brax, however, can easily adjust his approach.

"I'll ask Master Braxton." She nods, so I approach Brax, introduce them, and I leave, satisfied, watching as Brax leads her to the lobby to set ground rules before they scene. He can be a wiseass but he's a good guy.

My phone buzzes in my pocket.

Diana. *Feeling a little risqué, sir.*

And just that quickly, the demands of the club, the noises and sounds around me fade.

Yeah? Why is that?

Had some tequila.

Last time you had tequila, you keyed my car. Just thinking about punishing her sweet ass for that transgression makes my cock twitch.

I'm home, no danger of that now. Is it okay if I give you good thing number six? It's naughty.

Hmmm, let me think about that...

hahaha I can almost see her rolling her eyes.

All ears.

I... am very... very...

Yes? I chuckle to myself, as it appears she's either chickening out or is leading me on, but the teasing makes my dick grow hard. Jesus.

Flexible.

I burst out laughing.

Flexible?

Yep. Pilates. Yoga. You know.

I don't, but I believe you. Thank you for that, Diana. I'll have to put that to the test. ;)

Please do! Haha

A warmth floods my chest.

Ok, I've put Chad to bed and now I'm calling it a night myself.

I sigh, wishing I could go to her.

Sleep well, honey. xx

CHAPTER 13

I'VE MANAGED to hold down fluids now for twenty-four hours. Chad picked up some vicious stomach bug at school, has been down for the count for four days straight, and graciously gave it to me. We ordered groceries online and have finally pulled through. What sucks is it's now been a full week since I've seen Tobias. We've kept in touch, and he *almost* came to see me to help when I was sick, but I made him keep his distance. He compromised by leaving Gatorade and popsicles at my door. I would've loved to have him here, watching over me. I want to crawl on his lap and have him hold me. But he's got shit to do, and it's important I not screw that up.

He texts me and calls every day, and it's been almost a blessing, being sick like this, because he's proving the kind of guy he is. Funny. Sweet. Protective. He makes me smile, and I miss him. And he's been asking to see Chad, too. I need to see him again.

I'm reading his text from the night before, but still, I don't really understand his… attention.

Sleep well, honey xx is the normal text.

It's just not something a girl like me gets used to, even if he ends every night with the same sweet message.

Ok so maybe... *some girls* get used to it. But not me.

I look at my phone before I brush my teeth. Again, when I get into my pajamas, and again when I slide under the covers in bed. I replay his messages. I wait for his call. And when I wake in the morning, I smile as a new, "good morning" message comes in.

Morning, beautiful. Did you sleep well?

Not as well as when he's by my side but yes, I did.

I did, thanks. You?

Not so much. Got another disturbing call from NYPD, but I can fill you in later. Please be careful. Don't come to Verge unless I bring you, okay?

I frown. That's not what I'm expecting to hear, and this news makes my skin prickle. *Yes, of course.*

Thank you. But that wasn't the correct response.

My cheeks flame. *Yes, sir.*

Very good. May I call? Do you feel well enough to talk?

Yes! Yes, sir. :)

A few seconds later, my cell rings. "Good morning," I greet.

"Hey, honey." His deep voice instantly soothes me. "What do you have going on today?"

"Well, I've got a client at noon I'm meeting for lunch to discuss the floor plans for their new estate on the upper east side. They're pretty high-powered and willing to spend a good deal on making their place exactly what they want, so I'll spend a lot of time with them this afternoon."

"Sounds good. Chad already at school?"

"No, he gets the bus in about half an hour." I stretch and get out of bed. "Gotta make sure he's up and dressed. Over breakfast I'll talk to him and let you know what he thinks about the movies?"

"Perfect. Do you have time to meet me for coffee before your lunch?"

I feel like I'm a high schooler and the varsity football captain had just asked her on a first date.

"Yes!" God, do I have to sound so eager? Tamping down my excitement, I amend. "Would love that. Where do you want to meet?"

"I'd rather pick you up, and we can go to the bookstore around the corner from Verge, Books and Cups?"

"Never been there but sure."

"Ok, see you at ten? Does that work?"

"Sure." Since I do most of my work from home unless meeting with clients, that's perfect.

"Later, babe."

"Later."

I disconnect the call and push myself out of bed, smiling as I dress. "Chad, honey? Are you awake?" I call into the other room, and don't hear a response, but I hear the water running in the bathroom. "You in there, Chad?"

"Yeah," he says through the door.

"I'll make you breakfast."

I go to the kitchen and make myself coffee, remembering the coffee Tobias made me. I smile to myself, as the hot liquid pours into my cup, the smell filling my senses. The door buzzes.

Tapping the speaker, I talk into it, glancing at the clock. Way too early for Tobias. "Yes?"

"It's me, Bea. Lemme in! I come bearing gifts."

I hit the buzzer and go back to making coffee when the knock comes at the door. Chad emerges from the bathroom.

"That's your Aunt Beatrice. Let her in?"

Nodding, he opens the door.

"Hey, sweetie," Beatrice says, holding a pastry box marked *Tulio's*.

"It's not even fair, you getting donuts on the way back from yoga," I chide.

"I think it's super fair," Chad says, opening up the lid and grinning as he snags the vanilla-frosted.

I ruffle his hair as I make my way over to the table with my coffee and snag a chocolate-covered donut. "God, this looks amazing. I'm starving." I take a bite and it tastes delicious after living on saltine crackers and water for days.

Beatrice sits at the dining room table and takes a sip out of the water bottle she perpetually lugs around with her, before she grabs a glazed donut. "I'm feeling like a splurge."

I wink at her and sip my coffee. "Chad, I spoke with Tobias last night." Bea sits up, paying attention. Naturally. "He asked if we could go to the NYC kids' film festival. Starts this week."

Chad frowns at his donut. "Outside? In the cold?"

"No, it's inside."

"Will there be lots of people there?"

"Likely, yes."

He chews his donut thoughtfully. "But you'll be there, and Tobias, too? So I can sit between you?"

"Yes."

"If he's there, I'll go." I feel my eyes widen. He never agrees to anything so readily.

"Alrighty, then, I'll let him know."

"You gonna text him?"

"No, I'm meeting him for coffee."

"Really," Beatrice notes, but I ignore her. I glance at the clock, and usher Chad along with his bag and coat, to catch the bus. I run back upstairs a few minutes later, wrapped in a coat and shivering.

"My *God* it's cold out there."

Beatrice had cleaned up the donuts and is sitting with her feet tucked under her on the couch.

"Glad you decided to heat things up," She quips.

I roll my eyes.

"Sooo." Beatrice continues. "You and Tobias are going to the movies. And he wants to bring Chad? *And* you're meeting him for coffee? Have you... found a way to figure out how you're going to settle what you owe him?"

I swallow and push my lips together to keep my face sober. It's so tempting to squeal like a little girl to my bestie. "I... may have already settled that expense."

Beatrice's brows shoot up. "You *what?* Did you... no. I know you didn't have the money. So how did you... *Diana!"*

"Whatever you're thinking, it's probably wrong. I didn't, like, suck his cock or spread my legs for him. Well...."

"Diana!"

"I... didn't do it for *money.* I mean the spreading my legs part. I haven't gotten to the sucking cock part." I shake my head. "My *God,* the shit you make me say."

"I didn't make you say anything! You *slept* with him. Already?"

"Yes, and it was amazing, so shut up. But that isn't how I paid for the... um... damage."

Beatrice's brows draw together and her voice hardens. "Girl? *Spill."*

"Okay, so he made me an offer and I, um, took it. I... took a spanking as punishment and it wiped my slate clean, and then it turned me way on, so we started getting it on but then, douchebag Billy stepped in as you know, so we had to postpone the, um, getting it on part, but then we did and it was amazing. And I have zero regrets. Zero. I don't even regret keying his car. Well, like in a way maybe I do because that was still a shit thing to do, but... well, it brought us together." I'm out of breath with this rapid explanation.

"My God. You're at the stammering fixation stage! Did you think of him when you woke up?"

"Well, yes."

"Last thought before you went to bed?"

"Maybe."

"And at any point this morning," Beatrice continues, probing me with an intense gaze as she crosses her arms on her chest, "Did an inanimate object of some type make you think of him?"

I remember the coffee. "Well… uh, yeah."

Beatrice sits back and shakes her head. "Girl, you're *past* the stammering fixation stage and you've moved head over heels into the *infatuation stage.*"

I can't help but sigh. "Shit. You're right."

"Wait, you think this is a bad thing?"

"Well yeah. I've jumped so quickly into my last relationships, and I don't want to make the same mistakes I've made before."

"Has he given you *reason* to feel this way?"

I think of our interactions since we've met. "He's made me text him things I like about myself and told me if I said another self-deprecating remark, he would… I was… like, in trouble."

"Ooooh. I like that." Beatrice leans in on her knees. "Did the spanking hurt? *God,* I want a spanking."

I snort. "Yes, but it was super-hot. And don't expect me to show you my ass every time."

Beatrice waves her hand. "Seen enough of your ass."

"As besties should," I snort, finishing off my coffee. "Okay, Bea. Thanks for the donuts. Gotta get prepped for my lunchtime client."

"…and your mid-morning hottie. I get it. Listen, Diana."

She stands and her gaze softens. "I care about you. Talk to me. I'll help you make whatever decisions you need to, and help you not go too fast too soon. Okay?"

Impulsively, I wrap my arms around Beatrice's neck.

"Thanks, babe," I whisper. I pull away, suddenly remembering something Tobias said the night before. "You know, Tobias has a friend who's a detective. And he's also a member of the club."

"Realllly."

"Yep. I'll find out more today and let you know?"

Beatrice shakes her head. "Find out if his friend is hot. If you come back and don't give me that very important piece of information, *I'll* spank your ass."

"Lovely. Getting dommed on every side now."

Beatrice blows me a kiss and takes her leave. I get ready for the day, wishing that I'd asked Beatrice to stay long enough to pick out what I'm wearing. In the end, I choose a typical outfit I'd wear to meet any client in the frigid weather: a pair of knee-high boots with black leggings and a patterned tunic top in golds and browns made of a soft, warm fabric that hugs my curves. I toss a filmy gold scarf around my neck, and fluff up my crazy curls, then work on my files all morning, preparing for my meeting later, until the buzzer in my living room snaps me out of my trance. Getting quickly to my feet, I glance at the time. It's already ten. That's Tobias then.

Racing into the living room, I hit the buzzer.

"Come on up!"

I run to the bathroom to check my makeup as quickly as I can, dabbing foundation on to smooth out my skin, applying a layer of sheer lip gloss, and finish just as a knock sounds at the door.

Peeking through the peephole, I confirm it's Tobias, and open the door quickly, smiling as he enters. He, however, is not grinning.

"Hey," I greet.

Without preamble, he says, "You always buzz people up without even finding out who they are?"

Oh. Shit.

"Um… if I'm expecting someone? Yes?"

He frowns and juts his chin to the door. "Shut and lock it, Diana."

I do, my stomach twisting a bit as I do, then I spin to look at him. He stands watching me with his arms crossed on his chest. He nods, then opens his arms and beckons me over. I approach him, wondering what he'll do. Would something like that get me... punished? When I reach him, he places his fingers under my chin, locking his gaze with mine. "I don't want to see you do that again. Understood?"

I nod dumbly. His eyes probe mine, conveying his seriousness, before he releases my chin and nods, letting out a breath. "Can't stomach the shit that's going on right around the corner from me, hate the idea of some sick fuck taking advantage of women. I might seem overprotective, but I get that way sometimes about people I care about."

The skin on the back of my neck prickles at the knowledge there's been another victim, while at the same time a small shiver shudders through me because he'd said *people I care about,* and damn, I want that, so much so that tears dampen my eyes. I blink them away quickly and swallow. Something seems to soften in him at that, his body relaxing as he pulls me into him and gently weaves his fingers through the curls at the nape of my neck. My hands rest on his hips as his head tips forward and our lips brush, the slightest glimmer of a kiss, before his grip tightens and he deepens the kiss, but only briefly. He leaves me breathless when he pulls back, and his mouth comes to my ear. "Missed you, honey."

"Missed you, too, handsome," I whisper back.

He holds my hand and steps back, taking a long, appraising look at me. "Wow. You dress this way for clients every day?"

I grin. "Well, yeah. I'm a professional. These particular people are high rollers on Wall Street, and have a lot more money than time, so they need me to handle things quickly and efficiently."

"Ah. So they're worth big bucks, therefore you need to *dress* like a million bucks?" His eyes crinkle around the edges as he teases me.

"Well," I say, "Lucky for me, you're used to women dressed in latex and leather, so it doesn't take much to impress you."

With a snort, he spins me around and smacks my ass before we leave. We go to the coffee shop, talking easily as we drive. God, it's nice being with him again. It feels easy. Right.

He parks his car beside a parking meter.

"Owner's a good friend of mine," he says. "You'll like her."

Her? A twinge of something that resembles jealousy hits my chest as he shuts his door and comes around to open mine. What the hell's up with that? I shove the jealousy away, surprised at the sudden vehemence. He opens my door and takes my hand, helping me out. A gust of wind bites straight through my coat and scarf, making me shiver. Without a word, he wraps his arm around me, shielding me from the wind, and ushers me into the entryway door. A bell jingles when we enter.

"Hello!"

"Hey, Marla." Tobias leads me into the main part of the store. "Meet Diana."

Marla's beautiful, and though she's dressed in dark-colored straight-leg jeans and a V-neck light blue sweater, and could easily pass for a school teacher or librarian, I suspect he knows her from somewhere else. She smiles. "Diana," she says. "Master Tobias." She doesn't even blink when she calls him *Master*.

I knew, then, how she and Tobias were friends.

"Cup of coffee?" Tobias asks, standing by a large glass display case filled with oversized muffins, golden croissants, and large slices of something that looks decadent, labeled "iced lemon loaf." My mouth waters.

"Please," I say.

"Food?"

"Oh, lemon cake. I love that. Where do you get your baked goods?" I ask Marla, as Tobias places his order and Marla pushes over two steaming cups of coffee and two plates laden with the delicacies.

"From her own kitchen," Tobias says with a note of pride that revives the jealousy I felt earlier.

Girl, grow up.

"No way! You bake your own things?"

Marla smiles. "I do. I love to bake, always have, and when I had the chance to combine my two greatest loves, books and baking, it seemed like a gift from the gods."

The door jingles again, and a group of three women bustle in, bringing in a gust of cold.

"Her third love is in the corner over there," Tobias says with a teasing glint in his eye, pointing to a large, elaborate display in the back corner of the store with a hand tooled sign that hangs above that reads, "Love knows no boundaries." Beneath the sign sits a pyramid-shaped display of glossy covers I can't quite read from where I stand.

"Sir, behave," Marla says quietly, but she gives me a teasing wink, before she goes to welcome the new guests. I follow Tobias to a circular area with an assortment of plush arm chairs and round tables in front of a real working fireplace that flickers and glows, embedded in a stone wall.

"I cannot believe I've never been in here," I say, shaking my head. "This is like... stepping back in time or something."

Tobias nods, obviously pleased. "My sister would love a

place like this. She's in college on the West Coast, double major, doesn't have a lot of time for pleasure reading."

"No way! You have a sister young enough to be in college?"

He grins. "Do I look that old?"

I snort and shake my head. "Well... define *that* old."

"I'm thirty-six," he says. "You?"

"Thirty-one. I had Chad before I'd graduated college."

He nods. "I'm fourteen years older than my baby sister."

"Wow, that's a huge difference."

"Yeah. And since my dad took off when I was a kid, and I was the oldest, my sister and I got tight. She looked up to me, and she didn't have much in the way of parents, so you know, I took care of her. We read a lot when I put her to bed at night, and she became a really big reader. In fact, she's studying creative writing at UCLA."

"Good for her. Did she get a scholarship?" I ask, then realize I sound nosy. "Sorry, I don't mean to pry—"

He shakes his head, his eyes sobering. "Listen, Diana. Things are moving fast here, between us," he says. "There's no apologizing for prying. You have a question, you ask. I've got nothing to hide."

I like that. "Okay," I whisper, wondering if I can really give him the same courtesy.

"She got a scholarship, but it's expensive out there. So I'm helping and she's getting some loans, too."

"Geez. That's a big responsibility."

He lifts a shoulder. "Nothing I'm not used to. I was the one in charge of three kids since the time I was a kid myself. Never really got a chance to be a kid and never really wanted to. It came natural to me, taking care of them. Teaching them. Just part of who I am. It's kinda why I feel so comfortable around Chad."

That explains a lot. "You said your mom lives locally?"

He huffs out a laugh and polishes off the last of his muffin before responding. "Yes." I watch as his stern face softens, and he scrubs a hand across the stubble at his jaw, his coal-black eyes warming. When he speaks, his voice is lower, almost reverent. "My mom's never left New York. Lives in a residence home about thirty minutes from here. Pricy, but some of my siblings pitch in." His gaze comes back to mine. "I'd like to take you to meet her someday."

Something tells me that would be a big step for him. He isn't an easy man to please, and the way he talks about his mama, I already know I'll like her.

"Explains a lot," I say.

"What's that?"

"The way you're all bossy. You've been, like, a father figure to your siblings, in charge of taking care of everyone and everything since you were practically out of diapers."

His lips tip up. "Yeah, pretty much." He leans back and sips his coffee. "So, your turn."

Suddenly, I'm not so comfortable here. "Me?"

"Yeah, honey. What about you? Got any brothers or sisters?"

"No. I was an only child." I look away, not liking this conversation but knowing it will feel better just to say it, have it out in the open. "Mom was a working mom, worked her ass off. My father was an alcoholic. Left my mom the day I graduated high school. Said she didn't need him anymore, had done his duty, and he left. Just like that."

He whistles. "What we have in common, huh?"

I laugh. It surprises me how easy it is to laugh with him about something that's always made me so sad. "Yeah, bonded over broken families, huh?"

"Shit thing to be bonded over, but yeah," he says easily. "What time's your client meeting?"

"Noon."

"Got you for another hour, then."

My belly dips at the possessive sound in his voice, and I suddenly wish we were no longer sitting in a coffee shop with no privacy. "Yeah," I whisper. "So these books..." My gaze wanders back to the elaborate display near the coffee counter. "Dare I look?"

He snorts. "Yeah, babe. Let's take a look." His eyes twinkle, and the way his lips purse, I can tell these are not the kind of books *he'd* read. "Not sure why you girls go for these books so much, but it is what it is." He takes my hand and leads me to the display, where I immediately recognize the black covers with handcuffs. A quick perusal of the covers and synopses confirmed my suspicions.

"Ah. I wondered as much. What, you don't like lifestyle books? BDSM not your thing?" I tease.

He growls, his eyes narrowing but twinkling.

"What?" I push, keeping my voice intentionally loud. "I don't know. These books are kinda fun. Lets a girl fantasize a bit." I pick one up and flip the pages. "I mean, you don't just *run into* a hot, badass dom *on the street.* You know? I mean, they're fast becoming an endangered species. Most supposed doms you meet on the internet are holed up in their mama's basement shooting off orders to their 'subs' and wouldn't know how to balance a bank account, never mind shoulder the responsibility of authority and leadership." I jump as a hoot of laughter from the counter gets my attention. Marla's grinning at me.

"You're so right, girlfriend," she says. "I mean, where do you even find a club around here? All those posers."

"Right? That's what I'm saying," I say, not meeting Tobias' eyes. God, it's fun goading the Big Bad Dom. "Damn near ready to spank my own ass," I mutter, loud enough for Marla to hear, drawing another hoot of laughter.

"Playin' with fire, honey," the low drawl comes in my ear, making me shiver deliciously.

"Am I?" I whisper back, swallowing hard and placing the book on the shelf.

"You stoke that fire well enough, you'll get your ass burned."

"Is that right?"

"Diana..."

"Tobias," I mock.

"Honey, do you have *any* idea how close we are to Verge? The *empty* Verge, where not so much as a bartender has yet entered?"

I turn to him then, the dampness between my thighs unmistakable. "Yeah?" I whisper. "Lucky for me, I know the guy in charge." I wiggle my eyebrows at him.

He swallows so hard I can hear the sound as his Adam's apple bobs, before he leans in. "How much time before you meet your client again?"

"Fifty minutes left, handsome."

"Let's go."

CHAPTER 14

It's maybe not a good sign that her teasing makes my dick hard as a rock. Jesus, what I wouldn't give to push her right up against the display and spank her ass in front of God and everybody. The very idea makes my hand tingle. I can almost taste the surge of adrenaline I get when I punish her ass, can almost see the red marks from my hand, feel her writhing beneath me.

She's addictive.

And fuck if she doesn't need this as much as I do.

Marla grins as we leave. I guide her to my right, my left side facing the street, before I grab her hand and lead her toward Verge.

"Pushin' your luck in there, woman."

"No, sir," she contradicts. "Pushing my dom."

Her dom.

"I don't like game playing," I bluff, feeling as if I need to keep a firm footing on some kind of control. She's beginning to make me unravel. "There are better ways of getting your ass spanked, you know," I say.

"Sure," she says, "like saying, 'Spank my ass,' in the middle of a bookstore. Yes, I'd be game for that. Or, say, pulling my skirt up and laying over your lap. Perhaps texting you a 'spank me' meme?"

A gray-haired woman with wide, round spectacles stares as she walks past us, her mouth dropping open. Just to give her something to talk about, I take Diana by the elbow and give her a teasing smack, which makes several passers-by snicker and the lady furrow her brow, literally picking up her skirts and scurrying past us with a disapproving glare. Diana sticks her tongue out at the retreating woman. She's adorable, but I make a clucking sound. "Alright, behave yourself, now," I order.

I can tell just by looking at her that she needs to know she can push me and that when she does, I won't crumple. I know the look by now. Submissive women who crave dominance need this from time to time, and Diana's no exception. I've likened it to a blind man finding his way in an unfamiliar room; once he knows where the walls are, his boundaries, he can move more freely.

Though she doesn't say a word, I give her a sober look as I unlock the door to Verge. "You know, I've been doing this a while now. I know that look in your eyes."

"Look? What look?" she responds, barely keeping the bite out of her tone.

"That *spank me, please,*" look. I pull her into the empty hallway and shut the door behind her. "The look that says, *dominate me.*"

"I didn't—I didn't mean—don't you—"

"Diana," I say evenly, holding her by the elbow and marching her down the hall, past my office, past the vacant lobby, and into the bar area. "You're an honest woman. Don't compound things by letting that slide just because you're embarrassed. You can get a lot of things just by asking. But sometimes? You don't know what it is you want, or need, especially when you're new to this. Lucky for you, or unlucky for you, however you wanna see it, I'm not new." We reach the dungeon that looks cavernous with no one else here. I release her elbow and point to the padded spanking bench in the center of the room.

"Lie over the table. Lose the leggings. And if at any point you want to stop, you say pink flamingo."

"What?" She suddenly has the classic deer-in-the-headlights look. But we don't have time to argue.

"That's your safeword," I say, my eyes meeting hers as I reach for the buckle of my belt. Her eyes go wide as I unfasten the belt and tug the leather through the loops, anticipation weaving its way through me, the sweet taste of domination at hand. "What are you doing?" she whispers, now beginning to really look afraid. "Tobias..."

Doubling the belt over and pointing to the table, I repeat the safeword. "Pink flamingo."

CHAPTER 15

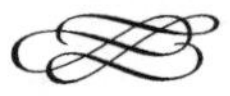

"I—I don't know if I can do this," I whisper, eyeing the thick leather doubled in his hand, the buckle tucked into his fist, with both curiosity and fear. "That's going to—hurt."

"Like hell," he agrees, which does nothing to calm my nerves. "Gonna sit tenderly on that chair in the restaurant."

I begin to tremble, frozen in place, and his gaze softens. I need this, but I don't know if I have the guts to take it. I want to, and I don't. He approaches me, taking my chin in his hand. "Do you trust me?" he asks. Looking into the depths of his eyes, so dark yet kind, full of warmth and a safely guarded tenderness, I know the answer.

Yes. Yes, I trust him.

"I do," I whisper.

His voice hardens. "Then go and lie on that table before I have to do it for you." Though he doesn't say it, the implied meaning is clear: *Obey, or this becomes far more real.*

I drag my feet as I walk to the table, my brain playing a loop of self-criticism I don't dare utter.

You're crazy.

You don't even know him.

The man's holding a fucking belt.

What kind of a crazy person wants to be spanked?

You said you trust him. Then do what he says.

When I reach the table, I step out of my boots, then slide out of my leggings, folding them neatly and placing them down on the small table next to the bench so they don't wrinkle. Standing before him clad in panties makes me tremble, and I can't even look him in the eyes as I turn to face the bench.

"You can keep your panties on. I'll handle that part."

Very funny. I'm wearing a thong. Super generous of him. And yet my sex throbs.

I hold my breath, steeling myself for what I know will be the first brutal lash of leather.

Pink flamingo.

Pink flamingo.

Pink flamingo.

I won't let myself get to the point where I'll forget to safeword or do something stupid, like let my pride make me wimp out. No. I'll take what I can, because that's why I'm here, but the second it gets to be too much, I'll safeword.

Gripping the padded table, I close my eyes, feeling the heat of him as he comes up behind me.

"Remember." His breath brushes my ear, his voice black silk. "Safeword if you need to. But try to take what you can. Sometimes we don't know how much we can take until we test our boundaries. Then we find out we're even stronger than we think." The breath whooshes out of me when he tugs my panties down slowly over the curve of my backside, down my thighs, until I feel the strip of fabric at my ankles before he gently tugs them over one foot, then the other. Bared to him and vulnerable, my breath catches in my throat. Then his comforting presence is gone, and he stands behind me, one hand on the small of my back. He rears back.

I tense. Then *snap!* The first bite of leather cracks across my ass.

Pain lights my skin on fire, breath hissing out of me and I go up on the tips of my toes. The sting fades quickly to warmth, then another stinging *whap* lands, followed by a third. The pain sears my skin, but it's somehow bearable, and though it hurts I feel myself craving more, harder. I arch my back and tighten my grip.

He whips me with the belt again, and I settle into the steady rhythm of him rearing back, then snapping the belt, on and on. He pauses. I look over my shoulder. Is he done? But no, he lets go of the double loop and wraps the belt around his hand, a tail hanging. "You're doing good, baby-girl," he comforts before he pulls back and lets another lash fly. The leather now wraps around my thighs. I whimper, but I need this, so I hold my breath and brace for the sexy-scary hiss of the belt slicing through the air before it snaps on my naked skin once more.

I lose track of time, closing my eyes, my mind is a jumble of incoherent thoughts. I can't think. All I can do is feel the pleasure and pain, my senses on high alert, the whoosh and *snap* and his heavy breathing. From behind me, I feel his hand on my lower back. "I could do this all day long," he whispers. "Take you to the moon and back. But I can't. You need to go, and for now I can only give you a taste of where this can bring us."

I turn to face him, both exhilarated and saddened it's over, watching in a sort of haze as he threads his belt back through the loops in his jeans and buckles it. I'll never look at that leather strung about his waist the same way again.

"You didn't safeword," he says, in a somewhat surprised tone. "I expected you might."

I shake my head, my words a whisper, the process of speaking after that difficult. "It wasn't as painful as I expected. And I... needed that. It was painful but perfect." Something in me shakes a little. It scares me that I really don't know what it is I need, or why.

He gives me a wry grin. "You weren't being punished, and you hadn't been warmed up. Either of those conditions were in place, I could've made it harder. I used the tail end as a strap. just let it land, and didn't put a lot of force behind it. Makes it easier to take. Still, you were brave."

My sex throbs knowing he could've spanked me harder and though my ass might not like a harder whipping, the idea is oddly titillating. And still, something is missing. I need something more. A harder spanking? Longer? Sex? I have no idea. Hell, it's all I can do to remain standing upright.

When he finishes buckling his belt, he gives me a tender look that warms me through, and crooks a finger. "C'mere, honey." He opens his arms.

Yes, yes, please. This is it. The missing piece. What I need.

I walk over to him on shaky legs, staring at the broad expanse of his chest, his stern but gentle eyes. I propel myself forward as if on autopilot. Dipping my head to his chest when I reach him, I rest. His large, warm arms encircle me.

This. This was what I need.

"Gotta make this short," he whispers into my ear. "You need a little aftercare, though. You took that well but a little reassurance might help. A strapping can be pretty intense." As he holds me against his chest, one hand reaches out and squeezes my ass, making me squeal.

"Still hurt?"

"Um, *yeah.*"

"Then I did a good job," he says with a chuckle. "You know, some girls don't like aftercare. Some don't need it. Others... it's what they're here for."

Where do I fall? I don't like the idea of not having this comfort after a spanking. My emotions have been played, my body under the control of someone else, and soon, I need to walk out of here and be all professional.

Hell yeah, I need this,

"This is like... the special sauce on a burger," I murmur. His body shakes with laughter as I continue. "Chocolate sauce on the sundae. Half-time show at the Super Bowl."

"Go on."

I grin against his chest, eyes shut tight, enveloped in his warmth and scent. "Heated seats in the car. You know. Fine, I'll go all cliché. *Icing on the cake.*"

"No, baby. To some, this *is* the cake."

Huh. Imagine that. "You mean to tell me that some subs go through that pain just to get to the aftercare? Can't you just... skip the whip and jump on his lap?"

"Skip the whip." His belly quivers as he holds me. "Forget *pink flamingo.* I'm changing our safeword. *Skip the whip.*"

"That's not a safeword. That's a safe *phrase.* Are safe phrases acceptable in the Big Bad Book of BDSM rules?"

"I don't know, I'll have to check."

"Didn't you write it?"

He groans, then his voice gentles. "Okay, babe. Time for you to go. You okay enough for me to let you go now?" And hell, if it isn't the sweetest thing, hearing him ask me like that.

I take a deep breath, then exhale it slowly. "Okay. Time for me to go."

Leaving the warmth of his arms is almost physically painful, but I take his proffered hand and let him help me dress again. Fully clothed, I walk with him out of the room.

In the hallway, I get a whiff of the smoke shop next door. Someone's lighting up in the employee parking lot, and my stomach churns. Everything seems so much brighter, stronger, more intense. But as we walk down the hall, the scent gives way to the clean, welcoming scent of the lobby, and then finally his office.

"I'll drive you to your client, and you'll get yourself home safe? You have a plan in place?"

"Perfect. And yes, of course."

"Chad gets home at three?"

"On the nose."

"Excellent. Then you text me when you get home, okay? I'll come over around dinnertime, we can grab food, then head to the film festival?"

"Why don't you let me cook for you? There's plenty of time later."

He smiles. "I'd like that." He spins me around so I face him, weaves my hair around his fingers, and tugs my head back, brushing his lips against mine, my heart smacking against my rib cage with the sudden heat that floods my body, the unapologetic kiss on the streets of NYC makes a bold claim: *Mine.*

I wince at the sting of my ass hitting his seat.

Mine.

"OH MY GOD. I met Tobias's friend," Beatrice hisses into the phone.

I grin. "Yeah?"

"He comes to get his haircut and I'm wearing yoga pants and a hoodie!"

"But you look sexy as fuck in yoga pants and a hoodie."

"Whatever! He came in and unbuckled his belt and slid the, like, gun thing off, and I think I had a mini orgasm. *Duuuuude.* I want that cop to spank me!"

"Well, perhaps that can be arranged. Lord knows I'm

dying for someone to spank your sassy ass. You know spankings hurt, right?"

"Stop! I'm gonna have another mini orgasm."

"God, you're hopeless. Oh hey, gotta go, Chad's due in five minutes."

"Sure. Just, babe? Let me know if you want to go to the club with a friend, m'kay?"

"M'kay, whatever that means. Later." I hang up the phone and go outside to wait for the bus.

I can tell from the moment Chad steps off the small yellow bus how the afternoon is gonna go. If Chad looks me in the eyes or allows me to hug him (he doesn't return the hug but it's a win if he lets me), it's a good day. If he doesn't meet my eyes or pushes my hands away, I steel myself for the night ahead.

When he storms off the bus and pushes my arms off him, my stomach lurches angrily. I close my eyes with the sudden tears that *will* surface.

Shit.

"Hey, honey," I begin.

Without responding, he slams his bag on the couch and heads to his room. Though I have a rule about where his bag goes when he gets home, and I've worked my ass off establishing a routine that would help him remember, I know this isn't a battle I want to face when he's in one of his moods.

Biting my lip, I pause in the hallway before I go to his room. Anything might have set him off.

I listen to the sounds on the other side of Chad's door as I stand in the hall. A click and then the hum of a video game console whirring tells me he's fired up his game. I sigh. There's a rule about that, too. I know he takes solace in the gaming system in his room, but he's supposed to have a snack with me first, show me the homework he might have, and then he can game before dinner.

He's pushing the rules.

My phone rings. Pulling my phone out of my bag, I recognize the incoming call and sigh, taking it into the bathroom and shutting the door. His teacher only calls me when it's something important.

"Hello?"

"Hi, Diana. It's Cindy."

I've been on a first-name basis with Chad's teacher since September.

"Hi, Cindy. I can tell by the way he got off the bus he didn't have a good day."

I hear a sigh on the other end of the phone. "I'm sorry to tell you, but yes. He was teasing another child during recess. From what I can gather, it was only in good fun, but you know he doesn't always know when too much is too much."

"I know." He tries hard to fit in with the other kids but often misses social cues, though his therapist and I work with him, and his teachers do, too. Role playing with him, and discussing social skills, he still sometimes pushes things too far with other kids, who are less understanding.

"So, the other child, who has some pretty serious anger issues, emptied Chad's bag into the coat room closet."

"Oh no."

My voice drops to a whisper. Chad's religious about making sure his bag is packed the way he likes it. He even lines up his pencils and pens by color, alphabetically sorting his folders by subject. His *Avengers* backpack is his pride and joy. If anything in his bag is out of place, he often tics.

"I'm sorry I didn't call you earlier. We had a fire drill at school today, and, as you can imagine… I have some students who don't handle those very well."

I pinch my fingers at the bridge of my nose. My son is one of them.

"I tried my best, as did my aide, in helping him rearrange his bag, but just around the time when we got him settled, the first fire alarm went off. And honestly, shortly after that it was time to get going home, and he was pretty wound up by then."

Oh, God. Sirens terrify him.

I let out a shuddering breath. "Hey, thanks for letting me know."

"Any time. Again, I'm sorry I didn't call earlier."

"No, you're fine. I get it. There's only so much you can do."

"Good luck. I hope he has a good night, and tell him I'm really proud of how he recited his Spanish today. He did an amazing job. *And* that I've never seen a kid read through *Harry Potter* so fast. He might even be getting a letter from Hogwarts this summer."

I smile wanly. "I'll tell him. Thanks, Cindy," I say, my voice pregnant with meaning.

"Any time," Cindy replies, and I hang up the phone.

I square my shoulders and approach Chad's room, but my phone buzzes once more.

It's Tobias. *Hey, honey. Leaving here in about an hour so we can make dinner before we need to go. Sound good?*

Great. How am I ever going to help Chad prepare for dinner with an almost stranger and a movie festival?

Sounds good but I haven't had a chance to pick up food yet.

No problem, got it covered. Does Chad like ravioli? Bread? Meatballs?

Loves them, I reply. One crisis avoided.

All set then. See you in an hour.

Great. See you then. I hope he can't "hear" the sarcasm in my tone.

I shove the phone in my pocket and knock on the bedroom door before I open it.

"Not talking," Chad spits out, his teeth clenched. "I don't want to talk."

Lovely.

"We need to talk," I insist, watching his reaction. If I push too hard, he might meltdown, and I don't know if I can handle that right now.

"No," he says staunchly, his fingers moving deftly over the controller in his hand, eyes riveted to the screen.

"I talked to your teacher. She told me what happened today."

"I don't want to talk!"

"Hey, no need to scream, buddy. You need some downtime, cool. I'll let you have that today. But you and I *are* going to talk and we'll do it in a way that doesn't involve screaming. Understood?"

His jaw clenches, eyes still on the screen. "Fine."

I draw in a breath and leave the room. A folder full of plans I have to work on for my new client sits by my desk. I have a little time to work on those before Tobias arrives, and I have to get Chad out of his room before then.

As I work, a little voice in the back of my mind tells me Chad will not be receptive to having company tonight. He won't want to leave. Hell, I'm not sure how I'll get him away from his console long enough to talk to him. As the time ticks by, I throw myself into my work, drawing out the plans and setting a budget my clients will approve of, so immersed in my work I don't realize the time until the buzzer surprises me out of my work.

Glancing at the clock on my laptop screen, I curse under my breath. "Fuck. I can't do this."

But I stand and square my shoulders, drawing in a deep breath and pushing the flash of doubt away. *You can do this. You do it every day. Chad needs you to teach him to handle this stuff. How are you supposed to teach him to handle it if* you *can't? Girl, you took a whipping with a belt today.*

I smile to myself as I go to the living room and hit the speaker button. "Yes? Who is it?"

I'm not gonna buzz him up and get my ass spanked for it, *thankyouverymuch.*

"Ahh, good girl," comes the familiar voice.

I grin. "May I help you, sir?"

From the other room Chad yells, "No people! I don't want anyone over here!"

Tobias speaks again. "It's me, honey. Let me up? About to drop this bag of groceries."

Smiling, I hit the buzzer, though my stomach clenches knowing that Chad is not gonna make this easy. A moment later, I hear a knock on the door. Peeking through the peephole, I confirm it's Tobias and open the door.

"Hey, handsome. Long time no see."

He smiles and leans down to kiss my cheek. The clean, masculine smell of sandalwood and strength blankets me as he rumbles, "Hey, honey."

I lock the door behind him and he walks past me to the kitchen, putting the groceries on the counter.

"No people over!" Chad shouts from the other room.

Great.

Tobias turns to me, his brows arched curiously. "Bad day?"

I nod with a grimace. "Yeah. Really bad." I fill him in. "And I haven't made him come out yet, but I need to."

He nods. "Not easy to deal with the meltdowns, but yeah, has to be done." He leans against the kitchen counter with his arms crossed on his chest. "My sister, the one I told you about? Practically raised her like she was my own?"

I nod. I like that though he's single, there's something we can share on this level I haven't been able to before. "She used to have *epic* meltdowns," he continues. "My mom, she was tired and busy and didn't have time to deal with her, so she'd give her anything she wanted. Mom went to work, but me, I didn't play by those rules."

I smile, already imagining the smaller badass version of the man who now stands in front of me.

"One night, she had a fit that beat all fits from the beginning of time. Had a world class temper tantrum over a TV show she wanted to watch. I said she had enough, she wanted more, I said no, fit ensued."

"Oh no." It's easy enough to picture the scene, and uncomfortably familiar.

Tobias shrugs. "Picked her up, brought her to her room, she tore every book off her shelf at which point I picked her up, sat her on my *lap* so she wouldn't hurt herself, wouldn't let her up until she calmed down."

"I can somehow *totally* picture this."

"I was bigger and stronger." He grins. "Guess who won?"

I smile.

"By the end of the night, those books were on the shelf, she slept like a baby, and next day when I told her to come for dinner, she came. We still laugh about that."

"You're big and strong, though," I say. "I'm... *not.*"

His eyes warm. Uncrossing his arms, he crooks his finger at me. "C'mere."

I walk to him tentatively, wondering what he'll say, what he'll do, and how I'll handle my son in the other room. Beatrice is the only one who "gets" it. Billy always gets angry at Chad's fits and insists he needs to toe the line which inevitably ends in a painful power struggle, and my last boyfriend was completely bewildered.

"Yeah?" I stand between his legs, planted like tree trunks, and his arms encircle my waist, pulling me close.

"Babe, you're strong, too."

"I didn't mean that I wasn't—"

"Who's the one who got him into the program he's in now, raised him alone while her ex took off, manages her own business, and keeps this place looking so perfect?"

Perfect?

"Well... me."

He taps my chin with his index finger. "Who's the one who has a lifetime of experience in this world and has learned how to cope?"

My voice even smaller now. "Me."

Do I really know how to cope?

He nods. "You're bigger and stronger, too. There's a reason you're his mama, and you're a damn good one." He pulls me into him. "Long day, it's easy not to want to face it. But let me ask you a question. How do you feel when I'm in charge?"

I sigh against his chest. "Good. It makes me feel safe and secure."

"Exactly. And even though you fight it, you pushed me earlier today to take control. Different kinda control, babe, but you need that from *me,* he needs this from *you.*"

What he says rings so true. I can't say anything in reply at first, but then he leans in and whispers in my ear. "And tonight? Diana, you're not alone. I'm here with you. I'm not gonna take off because your kid is being a *kid.*"

It's a damn good thing he doesn't say something else at that point like, "Do you want to marry me?" because I'm not quite sure I can trust myself to respond logically.

"Yeah," I whisper, standing taller now and pulling back so I can look at him. "Gotta handle this and help him process. I'm not getting into a power struggle, though. Billy did that all the time and it helped no one."

"Big difference from being *in* control and taking it," Tobias says. Then, with a smirk. "And that's right about where the correlations I drew earlier end. Because tonight, I'm totally planning on taking control." His eyes twinkle and his lips twitch, making me warm through.

Yeah, I'm down with that.

"Go," he says, leaning in and brushing his lips against the apple of my cheek, a whispery kiss that makes me smile. "Right here if you need me. I'll start cooking dinner."

I step away and squeal as he gives my ass a playful smack, then turns to the counter and begins unpacking the bag. Straightening my shoulders, I walk down the hall.

"Chad? We have company."

"Go away." The crinkle of the bags in the kitchen doesn't stop.

I draw in a breath and close my eyes briefly. "No. I'm not going away. You know the deal, kiddo. We talk, you do your homework, *then* you game. Today you had a bad day and I let the routine slide, but it's time you put that down and come here now."

No response.

Fine, then. I decide I'm going in. I turn the handle on the door, and my mouth falls open when the handle doesn't give. He *locked* it? He never locks himself in his room. Shutting the door is surprising enough, as he prefers it open.

Panic rises when I try the handle once more and find I can't budge it. "Chad! Unlock this door this minute!"

No response. "Chad?" Is he ok? The crinkling in the kitchen stops. *Shit.* I want to prove I can handle this.

"Chad!" I pound on the door, angry that he's going to pull this, but truly concerned about not being able to get to him. "Open the door!"

"No. I don't want to come out. I told you I don't want company. Go away!"

I smack the door so hard my hand hurts. "Don't you dare lock this door! I'll take away your game for a month! I'll—"

"What's going on?" Tobias's deep voice behind me makes me jump.

"He locked the door," I say.

"You don't have the key?"

"No. It's one of those push-ones from the inside."

"Ah." He crosses his arms on his chest. "Easiest ones to pop open," he whispers. "Might be better to get him to do it, though."

"How?" I ask, throwing my hands up.

He points wordlessly to his chest and raises his brows, silently asking me if it's okay if he interferes. Sometimes, Beatrice does, usually with pleading or bribery that almost always works, but something tells me Tobias won't try that technique.

I nod.

"What's going on here, Diana?" Tobias asks in a loud, booming voice, clearly wanting Chad to hear.

I take his cue. "He locked himself in his bedroom," I respond loudly. "Which is gonna get him in major trouble if he doesn't unlock this door."

"Got it. Hey," he says, so loud it almost makes me jump. "You think he's okay in there? I know how to open the door."

The toggling sounds on the other side of the door stop. "Chad? It's Tobias. We met the other day. Not cool locking yourself in your room. Don't need to tell you, your mom's not happy. I'm giving you two choices. You open the door and we all go have the dinner I've got cooking in the kitchen. Your mom says you like ravioli. Might even be dessert in there. Choice number two, you don't unlock the door, I open it for you and then you face the consequences. Your call."

"I don't want to open the door."

"Fair enough. More ravioli for me. Diana, be right back. I'll get what I need to open the door."

He turns, and I can tell by the look of determination on his face, he's not bluffing.

There are sounds of scuffling on the other side. Then, "I didn't want company tonight!"

Tobias turns back to the door. "Sorry to hear that, bro, but your mom did, and she lives here too. No worries, though. You don't have to talk to me or anything."

There's silence, then, "I don't want to unlock the door."

"Got it. Be right back."

He starts to walk away, and as he does, I hear the door handle jiggle. "What are you doing?"

Tobias stops, projecting his voice. "Me? Cooking dinner and preparing to unlock your door. You?"

I admire how matter-of-fact he is. He never raises his voice. Doesn't back down. Means exactly what he says.

Nothing happens for a moment, then Tobias takes a credit card out of his wallet and heads to the door. He says in an aside to me, "Your call, babe, but my kid locked me out of his room, that door would lose the lock, and that gaming system would be mine."

"Totally."

But before he slides the card through and unlocks the door, I hear a pop and the door flings open with a somewhat startled-looking Chad standing on the other side. "How do you open a lock?" He doesn't seem angry, anymore, just curious.

"We can talk about that after," I say, walking past him into his room. "Games are mine until you finish your schoolwork and eat dinner. Do all those things with a convincing apology, and I'll consider giving it back." I turn to face him. "You do not *ever* lock your door again."

He opens his mouth as if to protest, his eyes flashing at me, but Tobias speaks up, his arms crossed on his chest. "Seems reasonable to me." He shakes his head. "Consider yourself lucky, man, you get another chance of getting that back." He says it in a way that somehow both underscores he has my back, yet sympathizes with Chad. "Dinner won't take much longer. Wanna help?"

Chad blinks, looks at me, then back to Tobias. "Yeah," he says. "But first can you show me how you unlock doors?"

Tobias chuckles and claps Chad on the back. I freeze. Chad *hates* when people he doesn't know touch him. It's resulted in epic meltdowns in the past. But he seems to like Tobias.

"Yeah, I'll help you cook dinner." He turns to me. "But I am *not* going to any stupid film festival, and you can't make me."

"Whoa, now." Tobias holds up a hand, his voice sharper. "I'm a full-grown man and I don't talk to your mother that way. Why don't you try that again?"

Though part of me chafes at the correction, I know my son *needs* the example of a good man, and I'm doing Chad no favors by babying him.

Chad looks at him, then me. "I really don't want to go tonight."

"Fine with me, baby," I say, my eyes going to Tobias, who nods.

"Fine by me, too, could do our own film festival right here."

Chad grins and walks behind Tobias as he goes to the kitchen. I follow them, wondering if what I'm seeing is really happening. I shoot a quick text to Beatrice.

OMG. Chad locked himself in his room and was on the verge of an epic meltdown and Tobias stepped in. Got him to come out, and now he's helping him cook dinner.

A second later Beatrice responds. *That is the sexiest thing I've heard all week.*

Right?

Hold on to that one, babe. KEEPER. Keep. Er.

I shove my phone into my pocket, and look to my boy, standing beside Tobias who's just made him laugh, Chad's eyes alight.

What's happening here? The relief I felt a moment ago evaporates. I have to be careful. My stomach twists with nerves, afraid of what could go wrong. Am I doing the right thing?

I let out a shuddering breath.

There are now two hearts at stake.

CHAPTER 16

"Do not let go of that headboard," I order.

It's a full week later, and I've made good on my promise of taking control, her reaction so visibly pleased, it's all I can do not to fuck her up against the wall of my office when she pays me a surprise visit. I haven't, though, not immediately. I took care of business at my desk with a raging hard-on, then somehow made it to the private room earmarked as mine.

"God," she moans, holding onto the headboard in the private room tucked away in the back of Verge, her knuckles white. I've had this room custom-furnished, the small fridge stocked with her favorite drinks and snacks so I can ease her back to reality after a scene.

"You let go," I say, working her from behind, a supple leather strap between her legs building friction as I tug back and forth, "I'll take my belt to your ass again. Last time that happened you weren't singin' my praises, honey."

She'd lost her temper with me four days prior, after a shit day with her son and the babysitter showing up late making *her* late, and I had been doing up paperwork in my office.

The girl needed her temper taken down a notch. My repeated admonitions to settle didn't have an effect on her, and once I was done with my work, I'd taken her bodily over my lap. When we were done, she sat on my lap purring like a kitten, but not before she lost her jeans and my belt came off. I'd strapped her soundly, held her while she had a good, cathartic cry, then dressed her back up for a fun night at Verge.

"Ooh," she moans. "That's not fair. You're turning me on, mentioning your belt."

"You weren't turned on when I whipped your ass," I remind her, dragging the strap along her slit, watching her back arch as she draws nearer to climax.

"Not during," she pants. "After. Was turned on after."

"You're always turned on," I say with a chuckle.

"Can't—help—it," she gasps, writhing against the strap, grasping onto the headboard for dear life, opening her legs wider. "Boyfriend's hotter than hell. Dominates the fuck out of me, leaving me wanting more. Got that—ahhhh—sexy as sin voice. All he's gotta do is text me and I get w-weetttttt." Her voice comes out in a rasp at the end. She's gonna come.

I drop the strap and she tenses, but then I climb beneath her, grasping her beautiful ass that's hot to touch, her cheeks held tight in my grip, as I bring her sweet pussy to my mouth.

"Aw, *fuck, Sirrrr,*" she moans as I suckle her clit before lapping my tongue along her folds, rocking my mouth on her pussy in a move that makes her crazy.

"Yeah," I whisper against her pussy, just long enough to tease her, "Fuck *sir.* You will, baby."

My mouth returns to her swollen clit, watching her appreciatively holding the headboard as if it's a life-preserver. Hell, she's beautiful, her full curves in my grasp tight and sweet. Another sweep of my tongue and she's bucking, writhing, a guttural groan rasping against my ears as she comes so hard I have to hold her ass to keep her from flying right off of me. When she's settling back down, I grasp her thighs and squeeze gently but firmly, then whisper. "On your knees, Diana."

She scrambles off me and falls to her knees, belly down, arms stretched out in front of her. She knows how I like this position. Chest down, ass up, so I can smack her ass as I take her. Grabbing a fistful of her silky curls, I wrap my hand around her hair and tug her head back. Her mouth falls open, lips parted. I release her hair just long enough to push down my boxers and slide a condom on.

"That's it, babygirl. Nothing I like more than sliding my cock in your pussy and feeling your hot, freshly-spanked skin against mine. Love seeing my marks on you as I take you. Love feeling your hot ass against me when we fuck like this. Love hearing you moan, feeling that tight pussy before I come. Love how you push me," I hiss with a hard thrust, "make me earn your submission. Make me take you on." I push into her again. "Means more when I earn it."

"Fuck yes," she says, pushing back against me. I tense, holding onto her, and come with a growl, spilling into her, the power of my climax ripping through me like lightning, blinding.

I fall on top of her, slackening my grasp on her hair, both of us panting from exertion.

"Haven't done Pilates in a week," she says with a grin, her face tilted to the side and her fetching eyes locking on mine. "Don't need to. You work me over so good, I burn every single calorie. Of course, if you keep feeding me those damn brownies..."

I slap her ass playfully and pull out, grasping the hem of

my t-shirt and folding it, wiping her clean with the still-warm fabric before tossing it into the laundry basket by the door.

"Double score," she says, still clearly sex-drunk. "One for nailing me, two for the laundry."

Diana rolls over onto her side and draws the thin blanket up over her shoulder. This has become routine, her lying in bed in post-coital bliss, watching me dress. "Getting a little tired of you having to be Mr. Bossman after we make love," she whispers. "Would be nice to have you back in my bed, handsome."

Pulling a clean shirt from the small dresser I keep stocked with spare clothes for both of us, I wink at her before I tug it on.

"We can arrange for that to happen." I lean over and kiss the top of her head, feeling a pull in my gut I've never felt before. It surprises me so much I freeze on the spot, riveted in place, hands buckling my jeans.

She wants me in her bed. In her home. Wants to wake up next to me. And fuck if I don't want to be there, too.

A few days prior, she'd walked into the kitchen to see me showing Chad how to make homemade coleslaw, and her eyes had softened, warming.

In the kitchen she'd just stood there, eyes growing misty, and while Chad stirred the dressing, I'd taken her hand, squeezing. "It's so early, though. Things are moving so... quickly," she'd whispered.

"Never did care much for what other people say about time and shit," I'd whispered back. And I don't. I hate leaving her place. Dropping her off at home now is painful.

"Beatrice is coming tonight," she says, sitting up and pulling her panties on.

"Yeah?" I smirk. I've had a few occasions to meet with

Beatrice now, and like her. Feisty, like her friend, but even less reserved. But most of all, she's good to my girl, and that shit matters.

"Yep." She swings her legs over the side of the bed and grabs her jeans that are folded in a pile on a chair next to the bed. "I get to give her the grand tour." She turns to me, clad only in jeans and a black bra, and the sight just about makes me hard again.

"*You* are giving her the tour," I say, a statement more than a question.

"Yes, since my dom will be occupied with business-related activities. No worries, handsome. I've been soundly spanked and fucked into submission, so I'll behave myself."

I don't like the idea of my woman prowling about Verge without me. Some have gotten the memo that she is mine, but it's a large club with hundreds of members.

"If any guy tries to hit on you..."

My voice trails off, and I weave my fingers through her hair. I swallow.

"Tobias," she whispers. "What's going on?"

I shake my head. "Just don't like you being around other guys is all," I say. "Got an undercover cop here, and still, no one's found the asshole rapist who attacked girls on this street. Not good."

"Yeah," she agrees. "Not good. But I'll be careful. I'll stick with Beatrice and we'll go home together."

"Gonna take you home myself," I insist. "They can handle this place while I do that at least."

She smiles, her eyes warming. "I'd like that."

We quickly tidy up the room and lock it behind us. Diana's phone buzzes, and she glances at the screen. Normally, I'm not a fan of people checking their cell phones every twenty seconds, especially in the company of others, but I make an exception for her because if it's Chad, he needs her.

"Babysitter," she says, sliding her phone back in her pocket. "All good at home."

"Good. Hey, can you do me a quick favor? I need to check the supply closet to be sure the paper goods were delivered as planned, but I haven't checked the party room yet to see if the delivery guys dropped off the new table."

"Yeah, sure," she says. Since the closet is across the hall from the party room, we walk together. She heads to the party room as I open the door to the closet. After checking supplies and confirming they've been delivered, I turn to go, and almost collide into a girl in the hallway. She's the same blonde who approached me before, wearing bright red lipstick and her signature tattooed collar.

"Hey, Master Tobias," she whispers. "I was wondering if you're busy. And if not, are you scening tonight?

"Hey," I say gently, but firmly. "I'm sorry, but I can't." The door to the party room opens and Diana appears.

"All set?" I ask

"Yep."

"Ok, good."

Diana looks at the blonde girl, whose eyes have gone wide, lips parted the tiniest bit. "She's with you? Oh, God. I am *so* sorry," she stammers, shaking her head so her long silver earrings flash. Her cheeks redden as she turns and flees down the hall toward the back exit instead of toward the bar. I wonder how she walks so quickly on the high-heeled pink pumps she wears, but she manages it with ease.

"Oh no," Diana says. "Poor thing."

"Yeah," I respond. "I used to scene on the regular with anyone who needed it, and members here still sort of expect that. Haven't really made that as clear as I need to, that I'm not into that anymore."

"Yeah," she says with a smirk. "You were like the Man Whore Dom."

I take her by the elbow and give her a sharp smack on the ass but feel my lips twitch. "Didn't *sleep* with them, pretty girl."

"Yeah, you just spanked their asses, thereby making *them* want to sleep with *you.*"

I huff out a laugh. "Not so sure about that."

"Yeah? I am."

I shake my head, my eyes looking at the back door "Feel bad rejecting her like that, and I already did once before. I know she didn't realize I'm with you, but still. Takes a lot of guts to ask to be dominated."

"Damn right it does," she agrees. She ought to know.

"Hooked her up with Brax last time, didn't seem to go so well."

She snorts. "I don't know if I could take a dom like Brax seriously," she says. "He's all, like, muscle."

I smile. "That's a bad thing?"

She grins, shooting me a teasing look. "I don't know. Some girls like the dad bods. They don't like this chiseled ab thing. Like hugging a damn washboard."

"Unbelievable," I tease. "Giving me a damn complex."

Her giggle makes me smile, then we round the corner and enter the bar area. "Hey," I greet Travis and Brax at the bar. "You see Zack tonight?"

"Yeah, talked to him," says a voice behind me. Axle stands with Marla beside him. "Says he's bringing a girl tonight, wants to show her around. Hoped it would give him a stronger alibi."

"I see." I cross my arms on my chest and at the same time, both mine and Diana's phones buzz. We look at each other quizzically.

"Beatrice is here," Diana says.

I glance at my phone. "So's Zack."

Diana grins wickedly.

I chuckle, nab her hand and head to the main entrance.

"You know," she says, as we walk hand-in-hand, "with even a very modest budget, I could help you give this place a real face lift."

"Yeah?"

I've seen her work, and it is excellent.

"Yeah. Fresh paint job, some recessed lighting, a few minor touches here and there. Could be done."

"I'll think about it, see what Seth says," I agree. "Sounds good to me."

Her smile shows she's clearly pleased.

In the lobby area stands Zack, dressed in civilian clothing, his head shaved and wearing a scruffy beard. His faded jeans and black t-shirt will make him meld into the crowd at Verge, which pleases me. Beatrice stands next to him, her eyes twinkling at Diana. She wears platform black heels, skin-tight, black leggings that *lace* up the thigh and tie into bows at the tops of her thighs, a cropped white top that reveals her pierced belly button, and a short, black leather jacket.

"Okay," I say. "I'll have Diana show you around, you let me know if you have any questions."

Beatrice nods, her eyes bright with childlike enthusiasm as they walk down the hall. Zack stands taller. It's the first time he's ever come to Verge with a date.

"Thanks," Zack says taking Beatrice by the hand, making Diana's brows arch almost comically, and leading her to the lobby where they'll find paperwork if they need it.

"This way," Diana says. "Master Tobias? See you in a while?"

I nod. She's never called me Master in a scene, but at the club, she often does as a sign of respect. I watch her walk, her beautiful curls bouncing as she does, a skip in her step she's gained over the past month she didn't have before. She'll introduce them to her friends here. Though Zack's familiar with the layout, she's proud of Verge and wants to show her friend.

As I watch her go, something inside me whispers *stop her.* I stare, puzzled, for a moment, that the desire to stop her is so strong, so urgent, and I actually call out, "Diana?"

She stops in the hallway with Zack and Beatrice turning to stare and look at me with curiosity. I crook a finger at her, and swallow hard, not wanting to look like a dumbass. She's heading into *my club* where *I am,* with a police officer, for Christ's sake, and my best friends are strewn about like a horde of bodyguards. She's safe and secure, and nothing bad is going to happen to her. I didn't even allow her to drive here alone tonight, and she'll go home with me. Still, when she reaches me, I wrap my hand around the nape of her neck, tug her hair to pull her head back, and kiss her full on the lips, making her gasp into my mouth and her knees buckle. "Be careful in there," I rasp against her ear.

She pulls back and tips her head to the side. "Be careful?" She leans in. "Handsome, I've already scened tonight. I'm just planning on a glass of wine at the bar if my dom allows, and not exactly planning on tacking myself to a St. Andrew's Cross or anything."

"Yes to the wine," I say. "And good. I'll see you in a few minutes."

It takes effort for me to release her.

When I do, Beatrice turns to Zack. "Very nice, that move there. The hand around the neck thing? PDA? Big fan." She jerks a finger to her chest.

"PDA?" Zack asks. "What the hell is that?"

Beatrice rolls her eyes. "Public Display of Affection."

"I'll give you *public display of affection,*" he says, playfully slapping her ass. "No eye rolling, either."

Diana laughs as she joins them but I don't, the uneasy feeling increasing as she walks away from me. I take an involuntary step in their direction, then the door to the lobby opens, and they're gone.

CHAPTER 17

I LEAD Beatrice and Zack past the lobby and into the bar area. According to Tobias, Zack practically founded the place with him and Seth. "Drinks are served at the bar, and members must agree to limits set by the Dungeon Monitors or bartenders if need be," I say, before introducing Zack to the people I know around me "Down the hall we have a party room and private guest rooms for long-term members." It amuses her to pretend Zack has never been here before.

"Very good," he says, not at all amused. His gaze scans the room. Beatrice, however, is all wide-eyed and impressed.

"Wow," she breathes. The recessed colored lighting opposite the bar near the dance floor *is* freaking phenomenal, and I now know from personal experience the furniture, though functional, is super comfortable and kept immaculately clean.

"Yeah, it's a really nice place."

"Now I know why you want to hang here so much," she says with a laugh. "You give your babysitter the name and number to reach you here?" she winks.

"Mandy has my cell number," I tell her, with narrowed eyes. "And that's *all* she needs."

A heated conversation at the bar gets our attention. Brax has pushed himself to standing, and Travis stands with his arms crossed on his chest. Travis' eyes lock on Zack's.

"Zack?" he calls, his voice barely controlled, his eyes flashing.

Zack stands, immediately stiffening. "Yeah?"

"C'mere a sec?"

Zack heads to the bar, leans up against it, and Beatrice and I follow. Travis leans over toward Zack and speaks in a low voice. "Guest has just gone to the back exit. Says she needed some fresh air after a scene, and she saw some shit out back that indicated a struggle." Beatrice tightens next to me.

"Who saw this?"

Travis points to Marla, the bookstore owner, whose eyes are wide. "Get Tobias in here, *now,*" Zack orders to Brax, who takes out his phone and pushes a button with lightning speed, his eyes narrowed to slits beneath furrowed brows. A low buzz of curiosity follows us as Zack takes Marla toward the back. We try to follow him, but he turns around and gives us both a severe look.

"You do *not* follow," he says. "Get the hell back in there where it's safe."

"But I—" Beatrice starts.

"*Now,* Beatrice." She closes her mouth and her eyes widen, but she stands riveted to the spot as Zack and Marla go out the back.

"What the fuck," I mutter, annoyed. "I want to see what's going on."

"You? That's my man!"

I give her a curious look. "Seriously?"

Beatrice nods eagerly. "Yep. He's... I just...well I..." she stammers.

"I have legit, never *in my life* seen you *speechless,"* I say.

"Oh, shut up." But Beatrice's smile is pleased, her cheeks lightly tinged pink, when the back door opens with a bang and Zack comes back in, his phone to his ear as Tobias enters from the hallway.

"You girls go back to the bar," Tobias orders.

"Jesus, are they all the same?" Beatrice asks with chagrin, but I know that hard look in his eyes, and I know I'll regret anything short of total obedience.

"Let's go," I say, but then we hear Zack, and what he says makes us freeze.

"Barrel turned over, torn clothing on the ground, and a pink heel abandoned," Zack says. "Spilled purse to the right of the dumpster Marla saw, looks like it must've been out of sight." Brax and Travis enter the hallway. "Submissive at the bar says she came with a friend, thought she left to use the bathroom an hour ago, never came back. Tried her cell, went to voicemail."

"Pink shoe," I whisper. "That woman earlier who was talking to you..." my voice trails off as my eyes go to Tobias. "She was talking to you."

"The blonde?" he asks.

"Yeah."

Tobias turns to Zack. "According to her friend, what were the girl's specs?"

"Blonde hair, red lipstick, tattooed collar," Brax returns. "Claudia Bowen."

Tobias closes his eyes briefly. "That was her," he says. "Saw her about an hour ago. Refused to scene, explained I was with someone, and she took it nicely, but she seemed upset, embarrassed. Second time I've refused to scene with her, and she didn't take it well."

"Gonna go talk to her friend," Zack says, "and call in backup." He pulls out his phone, but before he speaks into it, he gestures to Beatrice. "Come with me. Need to get a read as to whether or not the girl is telling the truth. Need your opinion." Beatrice trots to keep up with his pace, looking scared but exhilarated. "We'll go to the dungeon," he says.

"What do you want me to do?" Tobias asks.

"Make sure everyone here's safe," he says over his shoulder. But as he walks down the hall and Tobias turns to me, it's like he just realized I'm standing there.

"Go to my office," he orders. "Wait in there until I come get you."

"What? No! Tobias, I can help you. This is ridiculous. You can't just lock me up like—"

He takes firm hold of my arm and marches me to the exit. "The fuck I can't. You do *not* push me right now, Diana, or this shit gets *very* real. Do you understand me?"

I turn to him, tears of frustration in my eyes. "But I can help," I insist.

"Diana."

"Tobias! Beatrice is with Zack. Let me help."

"For God's sake," he says, running his hand through his hair. "I will not argue with you. A serial rapist is at large, and preying on members of *my fucking club* and there's *no fucking way* I'm going to let *my woman* be at risk again. I not only want you to leave the communal areas, I don't want you set *fucking foot* in here again until we catch the bastard. Now either march your sweet ass to my office, or I carry you, and if I have to carry you, I swear to God you won't sit for a week."

His nostrils flare, his eyes furious.

"Okay, alright," I finally say, holding my palms up, feeling like a child who's been denied staying up past her bedtime. It isn't fair Beatrice gets to help with Zack. My adrenaline surges, my energy levels frenetic, and now I have to go and sit my ass in his office for God-knows-how-long. Alrighty then. Great.

I leave in a huff, conscious of the fact that he watches my every move, and head to his office with him right behind me. He guides me inside the door, then locks and shuts it without so much as a good-bye kiss.

"Déjà vu," I mutter to myself, picking up my phone and texting Mandy. I sit down, and my shoulders slump, suddenly exhausted.

All okay at home? I might be a little late.

All good, Mrs. McAdams.

I shove my phone in my pocket, and lean on his desk, resting my head on my arms.

So damn tired.

It's warm in the office. My whole body slumps against his desk, fatigued from the scene and my little spat with Tobias draining the last of my energy. My eyes begin to close after a while. I drift off to sleep.

The door to the office opens with a sudden bang, and I bolt upright, heart slamming against my chest. But it's just Tobias. His jaw is tight, his eyes clouds of thunder.

"Did you find her?" I whisper.

"Not yet," he says with a sigh. "But we found more of her belongings. Looks like she was abducted, and we're trying to get more information as we speak. We've got nothing." He sighs. "May have to close the club down for a little while so we can investigate properly."

"But you can't close your doors. This is your bread and butter! How will you survive?"

"We might have to!" he thunders, then stops almost as quickly as he's started. It's the angriest I've ever seen him. I don't like it. But he immediately apologizes. "I'm sorry, Diana. Listen, we have no choice. Financially, I'm fine. We have insurance that covers us in this type of event, and it's enough that it'll hold us through while we finish what we need to." He gestures for me to come to him. "Let's get you home."

I slide off his chair and go to him, taking him by the front of the shirt and pulling him close to me. "You listen to me, Tobias," I whisper fiercely. "This will be over soon. We'll find the man responsible. And once we do, this will all be put to rest."

He sighs, and the tortured look in his eyes pains me. "We'd better," he says. "I'll kill him with my own fucking hands."

We drive in silence back to my place, Tobias distant and distracted, responding to me with a mutter or grunt, but no real words. Finally, we arrive at home. He parks, comes around, and almost automatically opens the door for me. "C'mon, let's get you in safely," he says. He takes me to my apartment and does a walk through, which I feel is unnecessary, but I still appreciate it.

"All clear," he says. "Gotta get back to the club now." He waves distractedly to Mandy, then turns and leaves, never really coming fully present at all.

"Bye," I whisper, just before the door shuts behind him. Though we've departed many times before, this time feels different. This time the good-bye seems so... final. I tell myself it's only my imagination.

When I go to bed, I text him my good-night text. My phone lays silent.

CHAPTER 18

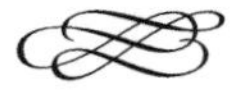

"WE FOUND HER, man. Dumped in the park. Homeless guy called in."

Zack's voice is both tight from anger, and defeated.

"She alright?"

"Fuck no. In a coma. Trauma to the head. Severe blood loss, may not make it."

Fuck. I wait respectfully for Zack to continue. "Fucked her over bad. Broken bones. Evidence of major sexual assault. She's bloodied, he obviously raped her, multiple times."

My fist clenches, gut tight with fury. "Christ."

I can hear Zack swallow on the other end of the phone. "Had to have been someone in your club, Tobias. Got to be. Three girls, now." He pauses, and his next words slam like an anvil. "That's three too many. We're gonna have to close it down while we investigate."

Though I already know it, the finality of hearing Zack say it makes the truth that much harder to bear. "Yeah. I understand."

And as I disconnect the phone, the reality of it all hits me with the force of a Mack truck.

She'd come to me.

After she'd come to me, I denied her, and she'd run out of the club.

I'd made her run.

If I hadn't—she might not have—I shake my head.

It's my damn fault. And fuck if I'll ever let another woman get hurt like that on my watch.

I watch as the moon outside my window grows fuller, then brighter. I shiver, but don't move, thinking, mulling, as the dark of night turns to the dim light of day.

No other women will get hurt on my watch. Never again.

CHAPTER 19

ONE DAY PASSES. Then two. He sends me quick texts to check in on me and make sure I'm safe, but he doesn't come to see me. He doesn't take me out.

I try to talk some sense into myself. *You're not doing either of us any favors by putting off seeing each other, you know.*

I stare at the phone with something between bewilderment and anger, pinching my nose in a vain attempt to alleviate the throbbing pain in my head. It's one week after the incident at Verge, and the club is still shut down, investigators combing it for any bit of evidence they can find, interviewing the nearby places of business as well, but no evidence is telling.

But worse, I haven't seen Tobias since that night.

He's texted, of course.

I'm sorry, Diana. I can't right now. I need to focus on what's going on here. And I have to keep you safe. I don't want you anywhere near here, and I'm here all day long.

All day long? He doesn't have time to come and see me for a cup of coffee?

God!

At first, I understood. It *is* dangerous for me to be there, and I know his priority rests with Verge. But after three days of not seeing him, I've grown wistful and sad. By day five, irritation grew, and now, day seven, my frustration has grown to full-blown anger.

I'm falling in love with him.

And if Chad asks me one more time if he'll come and cook for us...

A knock sounds on my door and I jump, startled.

"Mom?"

"Come in, honey." I put my phone down angrily while the door swings open, and Chad walks in.

As usual, Chad speaks without preamble. "Why haven't you seen Mr. Creed, and why are you angry?"

"I'm not angry," I lie. Even though my son often misses social cues, he occasionally shows perception that surprises me.

"That isn't true, mom," Chad says, plopping on my bed, his light brown hair flopping along with him. His hazel eyes come to mine. "I can tell when you're angry. I know your look. You've been sad, too. I heard you crying last night."

Aw, shit.

The night before, Chad asked if Tobias was coming to watch a movie with us, when I popped popcorn and bought pizza for an in-house movie night, trying to keep things special for him despite the ache in my heart. And I knew then that it was my fault for even bringing Tobias here. For letting Chad get to know him, and getting attached. I'd shot him another text, and he hadn't responded. I'd cried myself to sleep.

I reach for Chad's hand and squeeze. "I'm sad that we haven't been able to see Tobias, and I miss him. He has… a lot going on, and…" my voice trails off.

Chad looks contemplative. "Maybe if we go to the donut

shop he'll come in and then I can ask him why he's stood you up."

She laughs out loud. "Where'd you hear that expression?"

He shrugs, and doesn't laugh. He's totally serious.

I lean over and ruffle his hair. "Let's get you ready for the day. Today you've got that field trip at the Aquarium, right?"

Chad had been pushing himself to standing and now freezes. "No. I'm not going."

"Chad..."

This past week at school has been better than the previous, but he needs structure and routine. His teachers know this and will accommodate to a certain degree. His desk at school is always in the same place, his classes rarely varied with time or length, but sometimes they push the comfort zone a bit and it helps him learn to adapt. But, it isn't always fun when change is going down.

"I don't know where I'll sit," he says, panic rising in his voice as he stands in front of me with his fists clenched. "What if the driver doesn't know where we're going and gets lost?"

"Chad, the driver won't—"

"You don't know that!" He hates field trips, and for a brief moment, I consider just calling him in sick. I have work to do at home anyway. But then I think about what he'll miss by staying home, and how he really *does* needs to be challenged once in a while if he's going to learn to adapt. Constantly giving into his rigidity doesn't help at all.

He needs this from you.

"Chad, you're going on the field trip. You won't be alone, but with people you know. And you get to have pizza with the kids for lunch instead of packing one."

"I'm not gonna go. No. You can't make me," he begins, his voice rising in pitch, when the buzzer sounds at the door.

"I'll get it," I mutter, grateful for the momentary pause in hysteria. Great.

As I walk through my living room, my heart flutters. Would Tobias stop by?

"Hello?"

"It's me," says Beatrice. "Lemme up, chickie."

I buzz Beatrice up and go to the kitchen to make coffee, remembering when Tobias had stood me between his legs and told me I was strong.

Don't think about it.

"Chad, Aunt Beatrice is here," I call out. He walks into the living room and opens the door when Beatrice comes in carrying a large white pastry box, then without greeting her, turns on his heel and stalks off. Beatrice's brows rise.

"He's pissed he has to do a field trip today."

"Ahhh," Beatrice says, nodding. "Chad, got blueberry muffins here!" she hollers into the other room. Blueberry muffins aren't donuts, but they sometimes do the trick.

Chad comes storming in and plunks down in a chair, pulls open the box, and grabs a muffin, scowling. I watch him do this, and quickly meet Beatrice's eyes, sharing a look of concern.

I walk over, gently tugging Chad's plate away, and lean in, catching his attention. "I know you're angry right now," I say firmly. "But you are not going to be rude to your aunt and me because you don't want to do something. Now, you say hello, and then you will remember your manners."

He glares at me, his eyes going from Beatrice to me, but Beatrice only shakes her head. "Don't look at me, kiddo. Your mom is right. And frankly? Kinda hurts my feelings to pick up some blueberry muffins for you and you don't even so much as acknowledge me."

Chad looks away, eyes downcast. "Sorry, Aunt Bea. And… thanks."

I exhale, not realizing I've been holding my breath. I was preparing for a meltdown but was also ready to stand my ground.

"So where are you going today?" Beatrice asks, pouring herself a glass of water while I put cream in my coffee.

"I'm not going," Chad says stolidly.

I exhale, then breathe in once more. "Actually, honey, you are," I say. "And you're gonna be fine. You'll come home excited to tell me about the stingrays and sharks and penguin show."

"Penguin show? Sharks?" Chad begins to show mild curiosity. Chad has loved penguins since he was a baby, and is practically obsessed with sharks. "How do they make sure the sharks don't attack the other fish and mammals?" He asks.

I smile to myself but sober when I turn to him, needing him to know I'm not laughing at him, but amused that he has to make the very clear distinction. Not all animals that live at the aquarium are fish, and he'll correct anyone who makes the blunder.

"They keep them very well fed," I say. "But they swim along with the other fish and mammals so they don't attack. Scuba divers even go in and aren't attacked."

"Fine, I'll go," Chad says, and Beatrice and I share a quick, victorious look.

"Good, and you have money in your allowance to take to the gift shop after if you'd like."

I get him his bag and get ready to go.

"Mom?" he asks, as we go downstairs to catch his bus.

"Yeah?"

"Can you call Tobias? Tell him I miss him?"

My heart squeezes and I pull my son close to me, giving him a hug, just as his yellow bus turns the corner. Before he leaves he whispers, "You smile more when he's here." I stand, watching him, my throat clogged and tears blurring my vision, before I go up to Beatrice.

Beatrice sits on the couch, her feet propped up on the coffee table.

"So what's going on with Zack?" I ask her, loading the dishwasher.

Beatrice sighs. "Oh, he's good. They've got some serious leads but he can't talk to me about details. They're closing in, and there have been no new victims, but considering the fact that the bastard responsible uses Verge as his main target pool for victims, we haven't really given him much to feed on."

"Son of a bitch," I whisper, lost in my own thoughts.

"Heard from Tobias?"

My heart twists and I look away, unable to meet Beatrice's eyes. "No. Well," I correct, "If you count evasive texts? Haven't seen him. He won't let me visit. He hasn't stopped by." My voice catches at the end, and I can't look at Beatrice, not trusting myself to say more.

"You know he blames himself."

"What?" My head spins around and I stare at Beatrice. "For what?"

"For the victims. He's barely left Verge. Zack finally made him go home and get some rest, says they're doing everything they can, but Tobias is stubborn. Won't listen. Thinks those girls got taken on his watch, and he's... struggling."

Struggling? My big, strong, powerful dominant is struggling?

"God," I whisper. "I thought it was me."

"Course you did. You always do, and honey, it *isn't.* He isn't avoiding you because of *you.* He's avoiding you because of *him.*"

Whatever that means. Beatrice continues.

"You should go to him."

"Go to him? He'll spank my ass if I go to Verge right now. Doesn't want me anywhere near there," but even as I said it, my mind is reeling.

Beatrice stands and shrugs her shoulders. "Got my ass spanked last night," she says with an exaggerated wink. "Even have marks to show for it, which I never do, but woke up feeling pretty on my game and badass. Just sayin', honey." She turns and faces me, her voice softer now. "You've had a lot of shit happen to you. Shit people shouldn't ever have to deal with, you know?"

I swallow the lump in my throat.

"And Tobias is..." her voice trails off before she inhales deeply and looks back at me. "He's one of the good ones, babe. The *real* good ones. And you know, nowhere in this universe is there a guy who's *perfect.* And when you find a good one, honey, you don't let them go. Sometimes you *fight* for what you need. Sometimes, you have to chase it, wrestle it to the ground, and *claim* what belongs to *you.*"

He blames himself.

God!

If anyone knows what it's like to place the blame of something tragic on your own shoulders, it's me. How many times have I blamed *myself* for Chad's struggles? If I'd only eaten differently when pregnant, taken these supplements, given him the right foods when he was a newborn, been able to breastfeed like all the super moms I knew, or knew how to engage him at an early age and teach him to manage his frustrations, if I'd *never stayed so long* with his father, who'd only made a bad situation worse, or, or... whatever. The list goes *on and on.*

It's taken years for me to put to rest the self-doubt and recognize that *I do the best I can.* And there aren't always perfect answers to things. Sometimes, life sucks, and sometimes, it beats you down. But you keep on going, and when you get something good, you hold onto it. You savor it.

I put my cup to my lips, swallowing the lump in my throat with a sip of now-tepid coffee.

Beatrice comes to me and reaches for my hand, squeezing. "Go to him, babe. *Go.*"

I nod. I don't have a client today, and I've been so stressed with not hearing from Tobias that I've been staying up late working, needing to complete *something* and do it well. Needing to know I can do *something* right.

"Okay," I say with a quick nod. "I'll do that."

And though my heart beats with a frenzy, my stomach churning with hunger and nerves, I get ready, and leave for Verge.

CHAPTER 20

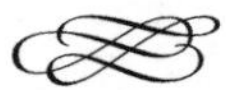

Verge looks eerily empty now, like discarded packages after Christmas, and my gut tightens with the loss. I hate that the tragedy of violence has come on my own fucking doorstep. When Zack arrives, we walk to the back of Verge, now lined with police tape.

Seth hadn't fought the closure, and he's been with me day and night, trying to find something, *anything,* we can go on. We pour over member records and profiles.

The members of Verge contact us constantly, wondering what they can do, how they can help, the tight-knit community bringing me a sliver of solace. One wealthy member even offered to have a temporary meeting ground in his expansive townhouse, but it violates city ordinance, and we can't take him up on the offer.

It kills me to step away from Diana. She's on my mind constantly, everything I look at here a constant reminder of her. The very furniture in my office reminds me of her. So I do what I have to, and push the thoughts away. If I distance myself from her, I'll forget.

I stare at the parking lot that refuses to give me clues.

Come and get me, fucker, I think for the hundredth time. *Let's see if you're so big and bad then.* I'll rip his dick off and shove it up his ass. I'll kill the son of a bitch.

Kill him.

"Tobias?"

No fucking way. I turn, startled to see Diana standing on the other side of the tape that loudly declares *DO NOT CROSS.*

But still. Seeing her here like this, her wild curls tucked at the nape of her neck in some crazy-ass bun with fetching curlicues haphazardly framing her face, dressed in knee high boots and dark-colored jeans, a long sweater-coat draped over her beautiful curves, drives me wild. *Christ.*

My anger simmers. I told her not to come. "What are you doing here?"

She draws in a breath, squares her shoulders, and her eyes quickly scan the lot before coming back to mine. "We need to talk."

"We do *not* need to talk," I contradict. "I told you not to come here unescorted, *ever,* and most definitely not when this place is a crime scene and under investigation." Though it kills me to say it, I have to. "Go home, Diana."

Her eyes turn stormy and her jaw tightens before she whispers a heated, "*No.*"

Zack clears his throat. "Gotta get back to the station for a few. Call me if anything comes up." He waves, takes his leave, and she has the nerve to lift the police tape and *walk across the line to me.*

"What the fuck do you think you're doing?" I ask. "I said go home."

"*No,*" she says again, reaching me now and when she does, she put both hands on my shoulders and *shoves* me inside.

What the fuck?

"Swear to God, Diana, you leave now or I'm gonna spank

your ass in a way *you do not like* and then *make* you leave and if I do, you will not like how that goes down."

But the woman is determined. Though I'm bigger and stronger than her by a whole lot, she can still move. "I said *no.* And yeah, I hope to *God* you spank my ass before I fly out of my skin with this need inside me, so guess what, handsome, I'm not going anywhere."

That does it. I wrap my hand around her bicep and practically drag her inside, yanking the door open. The door to the Smoke Shop next door opens before we set foot inside Verge, and one of the guys who owns it comes out, cigarette to his lips. He's tall and thin, wearing just a t-shirt and jeans, so he shivers against the cold.

"Find anything new, Creed?" he yells out, his gaze quickly taking in my grip on Diana's arm. He clicks his lighter and sucks his smoke.

"No, and even if I did I'm not allowed to divulge," I tell him, impatient to get her the hell inside.

The man's eyes go back to my grip on Diana's arm and his eyes narrow. "Everything alright out here?"

"We're fine, thank you, now go have your smoke and leave us alone," Diana snaps.

God, she needs a spanking.

I drag her inside, letting the heavy door slam behind us.

"You're hurting me," she protests, though I know I'm not. I've mastered the firm but painless grip.

"Am I?" I asked. "Or are you just trying to get away?" I let her go now that we're inside, and she spins around to look at him.

"Just trying to get away," she admits, her eyes narrowed slits. "You know, you don't get to ditch me like this. I thought we had something special. I thought I meant something to you. I thought my *son* did? Then you just... just... take off? Don't return my calls? What do you think I am, a fucking robot?" She reaches out to smack her hands on my chest, but I nab her wrists just before she does. I can hear her hurt, feel it in my gut, but she can't do this. I drag her into the room. *Our* room, still untouched from the last night we spent here, since we closed our doors.

"Didn't abandon you. God, it was a week," I growl. "I needed to get my shit together. And woman, you do *not* talk to me that way."

I push her up against the bed belly down while she fights me, but her efforts are in vain, and half-hearted at best. She needs this. My fingers nimbly push down her jeans, revealing nothing but the barest sheer thong and an ass that's way too milky white. I'll stripe that ass. Rearing back, I bring my hand down with a sharp *smack*. The breath hisses out of her.

"Fuck," she chokes out, but another hard smack has her up on her toes, her hands clasping the bedspread.

"Tobias! Sir! God, stop!"

"You need me to stop," I growl, spanking her again, feeling the sting in my hand as I slap her naked skin. "You fucking safeword. But you need this, Diana. *I* need this." I spank her ass again, then push her legs apart and dip my middle finger between her legs. My dick hardens, finding her so damn slick with arousal. "Jesus, baby, you're soaked," I groan, before lifting my hand back and spanking her again. "I needed to step away. Needed to get my shit together. Texted you every day, and did not leave you." I give her another sharp smack, then another, her ass a fiery cherry red now.

She barely struggles against me. She does *not* utter the safeword.

She needs this and she knows it.

I spank her until her ass glows red, before I grasp her hips and lean in, my mouth to her ear. "Gonna fuck you now." My voice cracks. "Jesus, I missed you."

She squeezes her eyes tight, tears leaking onto her cheeks. "Please," is all she utters.

Unzipping my pants, I push them down, slipping my cock out and sheathing myself with a condom. Without another word, I push into her, groaning as her hot, wet pussy milks my cock and she groans deep, a sound of need I feel in my groin.

"Need to feel you in me," she whispers. I wrap my hand around her hair and tug.

"*Yessss,*" she moans. "Fuck *yes,* sir."

Every thrust brings us back together, as I pound into her, the bed squeaking with my efforts. I shove my hand to her front, stroking her clit. "Gonna come for me, Diana?" I growl in her ear, working her up until she's bracing under me, her breath catching. She grasps the blanket and her back arches and her head falls back in a way that makes my heart twist. That makes me love her even more. The realization hits me hard.

I love her.

I don't stop stroking her until she's holding her breath. She grasps the blanket with her fists, her back arches, and she screams my name at the cusp of my own shattering climax. I fall on top of her, careful not to hurt her, but hardly able to bear my own weight.

She sighs. "I needed that. Sweet Jesus, I needed that so bad."

"Baby, we both did." I pull out and quickly clean us up with a washcloth before climbing onto the bed and hoisting her up in my arms so she falls onto my chest. I kiss her hungrily, our lips brushing gently at first, then with intensity, needing more.

I pull my mouth off hers just long enough to whisper a heated, "God, Diana. Not too macho to admit I fucked up, baby."

She smiles, our lips colliding, before she pulls back. "You did," she says. "But I forgive you. I forgive you because… because I love you," she says, her eyes showing that it takes effort to admit that. "And I don't care that it's not been long. Tobias," she whispers, her hand now on my chest as she speaks with conviction. "Lives change in a matter of *seconds.* People get pregnant. Babies are born." She pauses, her voice dropping. "People die. Words are spoken that change everything. So much can happen so quickly. And sometimes… sometimes you just *know*. And I just know about me and you."

I close my eyes briefly, surprised at the vehemence of my reaction. I look into the depths of her hazel eyes and know.

I owe this to her.

"And I love you," I respond. "And I feel like a dick now, but I pulled away *because* I love you. Because I can't bear the thought of you being hurt. I feel responsible for the death of those women, and I can't stand to think that anything would ever happen to *you.*"

She shakes her head. "Tobias," she says, her hand splayed flat on my chest. "Just because you *are* strong and protective doesn't mean you have to *always* be. You know? You don't lose man cred because you sometimes *can't be the strong one.* No such thing as perfect. And I love you the way you are, even if you're not like Prince Charming and Superman and Christian Grey all wrapped into one."

Jesus. I shake with laughter, but I not only know she's right, but this confirms she's the one for me because *she gets that.*

"You're only human, honey," she continues, shaking her head, her beautiful hazel eyes alight with emotion. "You know, all this time I'd decided that I'd never depend on anyone else to deliver me from all that fell on me. Never. I'd decided I'd bring myself out of whatever shit hole I found myself in. Deliver *myself* from the trials in my life. Then, for a time, I thought someone else could do it *for* me. Make me happy. Make me forget. But I'm changing that now. I am not going to deliver *myself* from the struggles I face. You aren't going to fix all that weighs *you* down. But together? Me and you? We're a *team*. And together, we *can*."

Jesus, what she gives me is beautiful. "Gonna put a ring on that finger," I whisper, my voice raspy. "But first, a collar on that neck, so any fucker who comes within ten feet of you knows *you are mine*."

Her eyes warm, then widen, and she says, "Oh! Oh my… oh my God, Tobias." The panic on her face makes the hairs on my arm stand on end.

"What is it, baby?" I ask.

She shakes her head, pushing out of the bed and dressing before I can stop her. I scramble to catch up, but she's yelling over her shoulder. "At the smoke shop. When the guy opened the door? I saw something glittering in the doorframe. Looked like a woman's earring? God, Tobias. When you said collar right now, it *clicked*. I remembered." She turns to face me, her eyes glittering with tears. "It was hers. Claudia's. It was her earring. And didn't one of the victims say something about smoke? They—I'm afraid—God, the department needs to go back and investigate the smoke shop further."

"Jesus," I mutter, grabbing my phone out of my pocket to call Zack as she yanks open the door to the room.

"I don't think so." Standing right outside the door, gun poised to shoot, stands the man we'd seen from the smoke shop. "Should check those locks better, chief. Been out here the whole time, waiting for one of you to fuck up. Suspected one of you'd noticed something, thought I'd listen in." He grins in way that makes my stomach churn. "Got more than I bargained for." He turns the gun to Diana. "Make a move, sweetheart, and I'll shoot your brains all over his goddamn wall. Got to listen to you beat her. They like that, don't they?" He stalks toward Diana, gun aimed at her. "They like it rough. They like to be punished. And you know what? They deserve it, sick fucks. So *I* punish them."

I'm torn between blind, red hatred that makes me want to hurt him, and fear for what he'll do to her.

He comes in the room and slams the door behind him, locking it with one hand, the other still training the gun on Diana.

My gut tightens and my mind races with possibilities. How can I stop this guy? How will I keep her safe? For now, we have to do what the bastard says before he hurts her. God, I'll kill him. I'll *fucking kill him.*

"Let her go," I say in a tight voice. "Take me."

The man laughs mirthlessly, pushing Diana to the bed. He waves a gun at her. "Take 'em off," he growls. "All your clothes. I heard him fuck you, damn near stroked myself off in the hall listening to you come. But you had yours. Now it's my turn."

I shake with rage, but control it, watching Diana's eyes come to mine. If I tell her no, she'll refuse, and he'll shoot her. But Jesus, I have to stop him.

"Now!" the man shouts. "You have until the count of ten before I shoot your overgrown boyfriend over here. One."

Panic fills her eyes as she grasps the edge of her sweater and yanks it over her head.

No.

"Two."

She looks at me in panic. *Stay calm. I'm not gonna let this happen. Just do what he says until I can stop him.*

But how will I stop him? The guy has a gun.

"Three. And you're too fucking slow." He points the gun at my foot and pulls the trigger. Diana screams, but he misses, the shot hitting the floor and embedding in the gleaming hardwood.

"Want me to shoot him again? Would be a shame. Need him to watch you as I fuck you, and so much of the joy in this would be lost then. I won't miss the next time."

"No!" Diana screams.

"You motherfucker," I growl but another bang sounds and Diana screams again. She falls to the floor and for one brief moment I'm afraid he's hit her. My vision is blinded with rage, I try to see why she's fallen, but I can't see. I focus hard, and from the corner of my eye I see her push something on her wrist, then tuck her arm under the pile of blankets on the floor.

"Get on the bed!" the guy screams.

"I can't believe you'd do this to him in his own club! This is *our* room!" she shouts, louder than necessary. "You hurt those women and you've got the nerve coming in here?" She's trying to distract him. Why?

The guy reaches her in two steps, rears back, and backhands her. I'll kill him. I'll fucking kill him for hurting her. She screams at the blow, and the guy turns the gun on me, knowing I'm ready to hurt him.

"One more word, I shoot you between the eyes," the guy growls.

The guy shoves Diana onto the bed. "Everything off. Jewelry. All of it. You do it in ten seconds, or your boyfriend gets it."

Diana fumbles with the clothes, shoving them off, when a noise sounds outside the bedroom.

"Motherfucker," the guy mutters, but the momentary distraction is all I need. I shove the chair next to the guy, hard, so that it topples into him. I pounce, tackling the man to the floor, a shot ringing out in a deafening roar. I grab the gun and throw it inside the bathroom, then turn and hit the man with my fist, the man's jaw snapping back. The sick fucker threatened Diana and hurt three other innocent women. He'll fucking pay.

I hit him again, and again, until the man's eyes are swollen shut and his body slumps onto the floor. At the same time the door to the room crashes open, but I see nothing, blind to everything around me but punishing the man who hurt us, who humiliated my woman.

I give him one vicious blow after another, wanting to maim the man, tempted to kill him for what he's done. He needs to feel the pain he inflicted on others. He isn't good enough to breathe the same air Diana does.

"Tobias, enough!" My vision momentarily clears to see Zack, pulling out a pair of handcuffs before he pulls me off the bloodied, unconscious body beneath me. "You got him. Jesus, brother, you got him. You don't want his blood on your hands."

With herculean effort, I sit back and allow Zack to cuff the man. I look to find Beatrice with Diana, rapidly dressing her. Diana's shaking. I go straight to her.

CHAPTER 21

"BRILLIANT," I say, holding Diana against my chest and running my hand along her crazy curly hair. "Using your watch like that to call Beatrice."

"I knew she'd be with Zack and when she heard my call, she'd know where I was and why I was calling. Thank God they were already on their way to Verge, or I'm not sure they'd have made it in time. Actually… no. You nailed that guy before they arrived. I'm not sure they'd have arrived in time from stopping you from killing *him*."

I just grunt.

We sit on a little loveseat in her living room. After a full check-up we were given leave to come home. And I didn't hesitate to come home with her, the two of us are now waiting for Chad's bus. It seems like it should be days later, everything happened so quickly.

"You okay, baby?"

She exhales. "You know," she says. "That was terrifying. Horrifying. And just plain creepy as fuck. But me? I'm better than I've been in a really, *really* long time." She closes her eyes and burrows onto my chest. I hold her close, kissing the top of her head.

"And *you?* Are you okay?"

I sigh in contentment. "Honey, I'm better than *I've* been in pretty much fucking *ever*. Got that guy behind bars. Got my girl back. And I know now, this is going where I want it to, you and me. Yeah, baby," I say, dipping my head to brush my lips on her forehead. "I'm good."

We sit in silence for a while before I speak again. "We'll get that guy behind bars for life. And I'm gonna talk to Seth. Seems we need a new location for Verge. Don't ever want to set foot in that place again, remembering what he did to you. Need a new association. Something fresh."

"You know, that's a great idea. I love it." She pauses, her voice dropping. "And I love you."

I'll never get tired of hearing those words.

I nod. "And I love you, Diana," I whisper. "Gonna make you mine in all the ways I can."

"You already have," she whispers, then blows out a breath. "I'm so sorry for the women who were hurt. But I'm also just so grateful we put an end to this."

"Me, too."

"Okay, time to get to the bus stop. He'll be here any minute and it scares him if he doesn't see me right off the bat."

"Understood. I'll go with you. Remember, we do things together now."

"Yeah, handsome. I like that," she says with a grin. "Together."

EPILOGUE

SIX MONTHS LATER

"Hey," he says, catching my attention. I'm standing in front of the mirror, turning this way and that, making sure that I'm fully covered. Tonight, Tobias has asked me to do a demonstration in front of a crowded room. We've opened the new location for Verge just this month, and his members have been clamoring for everything Verge used to offer before–demos, parties in the party room, in addition to the security, privacy, and comforts they've come to expect.

Seth and Tobias feared opening the doors to the new Verge would see a membership loss, afraid that the negative publicity they'd seen in recent months would affect them. To their surprise, it hasn't waned in the slightest. In fact, they're thriving. Their new spot is in a swankier location and brings with it a heftier price tag, so they upped membership fees. It worked in their favor, though. They have so many requests to join, they have to turn people away. Lucky for them, they have an in-house interior decorator who knows her shit. The place looks *amazing.*

No more long, dark hallway to get to the lobby. Now, the entry area contains an office and a community room. His office is tucked in the corner, and private, but the larger area across from it is spacious and welcoming, with comfortable furniture, good lighting, and all the information new members could possibly need. All who enter must go through the community room, show proper I.D. to the bouncer, and only then are they allowed entry to Verge. The entryway opens immediately to a huge bar, dance floor, leather seating, and small, circular tables for couples to mingle. We serve light food and drinks. Like the previous set-up, we wanted to keep things similar, we have the party room and dungeon offset from the main bar area, along with color-coordinated private rooms, but there is no back exit. We have fire exits only, and regulars must all enter through the main door and exit through the main door.

Tobias asked me to do a demo with him tonight. I've wanted to do this. Beatrice is seething with jealousy, as she can't seem to convince Zack to do a public demo for anything. Though Tobias has stepped down from scening with anyone else—he may be my dom, but I'll kick his ass, or at least try to—members miss his thorough demos. He asked me if I'd be game for one, and to my surprise, pushed harder than I expected. I agreed. I love to please him. And I'm a little turned on at the thought of a public demonstration.

Still, because others will be watching us scene, I need to look *good.*

I look in the mirror, watching as Tobias approaches behind me. He's got that look in his eyes that I can never quite identify, only one word coming to mind when he gets it: *hungry.* It is the same look he had when he collared me two weeks ago. The same one he gets when he makes love to me, betraying an animalistic possession he can barely temper.

I don't want him to temper it anyway. I like bringing out his fierceness.

"I'm surprised, sir," I tease, my eyes glinting. "You love me in the red corset top and knee-length leather boots. And yet you have me dressed for a scene in a BDSM Club in nothing short of a burka."

I'm teasing, of course. The long-sleeved top and fitted leggings fit me like a glove. Every inch of me is covered, though.

"No one sees you in that but me," he says, reaching me now, wrapping one arm around my chest, his mouth up to my ear. I shiver at his touch, his breath warm and sweet on my cheek.

I smile at him, my breathing slowing. When he touches me like this, it relaxes me. I'm conditioned now. When I feel my temperature rising, or I'm afraid of something, all he has to do is touch me—his hand on the back of my neck, a squeeze of my thigh, my hand engulfed in his, and my breath whooshes out of me in a gentle release. His hand presses up against my side, his torso pressed up against my back. He kisses the top of my head, then my cheek, and moves his mouth down to my neck. I shiver. He's my undoing and my fortress.

"Then why," I ask, panting now, "Did you decide to do a demo? You're so damn possessive, I sometimes wonder if you watch me when I sleep."

"I do."

I smile. I like that. I look at his dark, handsome face in the mirror behind me. Gone is the line of worry that once knit his brows together. He doesn't frown as much as he used to, but smiles more. It isn't just me, though. I think it also has something to do with the little boy who wrapped his arms around Tobias's neck before we left tonight. Chad smiles more now, too. He's thriving in school, progressing in his studies, and even initiating conversation with others. He still lapses into some of his old ways, but he's growing. Changing.

We both are.

Now that Tobias is an ever-present part of both of our lives, even Billy watches himself now, and Chad has come to almost look forward to his visits with his father. Though I miss him terribly when he's gone, I have to admit it comes with benefits. Those are nights Tobias pulls out all the stops, and the louder toys he has in his arsenal—his leather belt, the leather-wrapped paddle, or one of his floggers—comes out to play. I don't have to shove sheets in my mouth when I scream his name. We sleep skin-to-skin and revel in each other.

"You'll see why I want to do this shortly," he promises. "Trust me, baby."

And I do. *I do.*

He releases me, takes me by the hand, and he leads me to the dungeon.

I like this dungeon better than the last. It's larger, more comfortable, and welcoming. Tonight, a low buzz of anticipation greets us as Tobias leads me to the room. I'm thankful he isn't doing a *heavy* demo, though.

Tonight, he's demonstrating aftercare. The intimate, post-scene bonding that some of us crave so desperately, the closeness that forges necessary bonds of trust. Some days, I need that aftercare like the earth needs the sun. We've done a few public scenes lately, and his attention to detail was noticed by members. They asked him to demonstrate.

"You'll have to act a little, honey," he says into my ear. "Not gonna be too hard on you." He pauses, his voice deepening. "*That* will come later."

My nipples harden with the promise.

"Evening, everyone," he says, the room quieting at the sound of his voice. A hush falls over us. I bow my head, and pull a little closer to him, both a sign of respect and more, a need to feel his strength. "Tonight, my girl has agreed to allow me to demo aftercare. Simply put, aftercare often ends the scene, the time when the top assesses the mental, physical, and psychological state of the submissive. Frequently, during a scene, measured trauma is inflicted." He pauses, his voice holding the whisper of a smile. "Good pain, of course. But the more intense the session, the more likely the need for aftercare. For a submissive who enters sub-space, it's a necessity."

He turns to me, and his voice sharpens. "Turn and face the wall, Diana," he orders.

"Yes, sir."

Shaking, I face the wall and close my eyes, my belly dipping and a low throb of excitement coursing through me. It's the lead-up to the spanking I find hardest, when my nerves are on edge. During the actual scene, my anxiety lessens.

"What did I tell you not to do?" he asks in the tone that makes my breath shorten, even though I know we're scening. This is role play, an act, but I've heard that tone enough times for real that I can't help but feel momentary panic.

"Not to eat the rest of your ice cream, sir," I quip. He didn't actually tell me what to say, and it pops out of my mouth before I can stop it. Laughter bubbles up around us, but soon I'm not laughing as his firm, solid palm cracks against my ass.

"Do you think this is a laughing matter?" he corrects.

"No, sir," I say, gritting my teeth. It sure as hell isn't. He spanks me hard, and even though I *love* being put in my place, even crave a good spanking after too much time lapses, it hurts.

He pauses. "If this were for real, she'd lose the leggings, but tonight we'll pretend I've bared her and striped her ass."

Now *that* turns me on.

He leans in to me and whispers in my ear. "Pretend to be really upset."

I wipe my eyes, sniffling. He turns me around to him. "Sometimes, the emotions become overwhelming, and a bottom or submissive may cry. Listen carefully. Watch the cues. Holding him or her, reminding your bottom or submissive that they did a good job and that you're proud of them, wiping tears… you'll find what works for you. But don't underestimate the power of an aftercare session." He pulls me to his chest and smoothes his hand down my hair. He holds me, and stops speaking. The demo isn't anywhere near done. Why did he stop?

For some reason, I can feel him trembling. His breathing is ragged, his hands shaky.

Why is he nervous?

Then he lets me go and drops to one knee. I stare at him in confusion for a moment as a hush falls over the crowd. His voice carries in the small, intimate room. "There's another reason why I've brought her here tonight, to this room," he says, his eyes meeting mine.

It takes me a second to realize what he's doing, a cold nervousness and eager anticipation rendering me speechless until I barely eke out a breathy, pleading, "Tobias."

He pulls a black velvet box out of his pocket. "We met at Verge," he says, in a whisper only I can hear. "It was only fitting I ask you this here." He grins and opens the box. "Be mine forever, Diana? Will you marry me?"

The silence hangs in the room, every one of them awaiting my answer, but I don't need to think. I'd have said yes to him the first night he cooked in my kitchen.

"Yes," I whisper, not trusting my voice not to crack. Cheers erupt around us, Tobias grins, and slips a beautiful, glittering diamond ring on my finger, then pushes himself to standing and wraps me in his arms.

Beatrice and Zack make their way to us. I didn't even know they were here. She squeals and claps her hands, then pulls me in an embrace so tight I almost fall over, but Tobias rights me. Zack claps him on the back, and Marla pushes over a cart with a huge cake on it that reads, *She said yes!*

I laugh out loud, happy tears brimming my eyes. "And what would you have done if I'd said no?"

"Eaten that whole damn cake myself and cried myself to sleep tonight," Marla says with a grin. Beatrice cuts cake slices and hands them out, and I see Travis toss multi-colored glittery dots of confetti high in the air. Tobias will kick his ass for messing up his dungeon like that, but tonight, he doesn't care. They knew. They all knew.

But then again, so did I.

He holds my hand up like he's won me, and he's the champion. They cheer around us, the noise near deafening.

And it takes me a minute before I realize… I'm his prize.

THE END

BONUS CONTENT (opening chapter)

Beauty's Daddy: A Beauty and the Beast Adult Fairy Tale

Icy rain whipped my face and hands as I bolted down the length of Main Street. My mind a million other places, I turned the corner and crashed straight into the hugest, most arrogant, pissed-off man I'd ever laid eyes on.

"Jesus!" he roared, lifting the cup up to try to avoid spilling even more, but it was useless. "Watch where the hell you're going!" His deep voice startled me as he looked down from a lofty height, easily a foot taller than I was. So ashamed I could barely look at him, I was only vaguely aware that he looked familiar. He grasped his crushed coffee cup in one hand, a huge umbrella in the other, held so high over my head it did little to stop the downpour. Thick but well-kept stubble lined his sharp jaw, and black hair hung in savage, daring shocks across his forehead.

My mouth dropped open in horror. "I am so sorry," I said, looking around frantically but unfortunately there was nothing along the lines of stray rolls of paper towels or time turners that would help me make this predicament any better. There was just me, a sodden, furious monster of a man, and a few bashful onlookers who went on about their business.

They were smart. He looked ready to kill.

I inhaled, prepared to offer my most sincere apology. He towered over me, easily a full head over my slight 5'1" frame. His hands flicked off excess coffee, while he growled, in a deep, husky, pissed-off voice that sounded more like a growl than polite conversation, "You ought to watch where you're going. For crying out loud, you could've burned yourself." He grunted, attempting to smooth out his clothing, but it was no use. He was a sodden mess. "Did you?"

I blinked. Did I what?

His eyes lifted to mine, brows knit with a furious glare, his lips thinned. "Burn yourself," he spat out.

I looked down at myself stupidly before responding. "No…I'm fine."

"Good," he muttered. "But for Christ's sake, watch where you're going." He turned to leave.

"Mister — whoever —" I sputtered. "I am so sorry I bumped into you like that. Please allow me to compensate you in some way, pay for your dry cleaning, or —"

He turned a scornful eye at me, lips turning down at the edges, his eyes raking me over from head to toe before he scoffed. "You couldn't afford it," he said, before he turned on his heel and left.

My stomach dropped, and then I realized that I was now officially late for work.

"Annabelle!" So much for hoping that Linus, the overbearing owner of Diner on Main, wasn't in yet. "You're late?"

I frowned, turning away from him and hoping he'd get too busy to notice me again, when I heard a voice behind me.

"Do you have any idea who you just slammed into?" Lucy, the local librarian, was all about small town gossip, and knew every single person who ever set foot in any place at any time. She was even tinier than I was, with thick blonde hair pulled into a braid, sporting a short denim jumper. Perched upon a stool at the counter, her blue eyes blinked at me.

"No idea, Luce," I said, stepping out of my rain coat and shaking it off in the back room. "And I don't care. He's the biggest jerk I've ever —"

"Annabelle!" My stomach clenched and I barely stifled a groan.

"Good morning, Linus," I said as pleasantly as possible, taking my apron off a peg just behind the cash register and slipping it over my head as Linus came around the corner. Linus — a middle-aged dictator with wire-rimmed glasses atop his too-long nose, a thin moustache and a scant scattering of mud-colored hair across his head, frowned at me.

I fumbled to tie the apron in the back, when Lucy came over and did it for me, leaning in to whisper in my ear. "Don't mind him, honey," she said. "He's in a bit of a temper this morning."

When was Linus not in a bit of a temper?

"Do you know what time it is?" he grumbled, pointing up to the clock.

I can tell time, dumbass.

Releasing a shuddering breath, I nodded. "Yes, sir. 7:07. Looks like my lucky day?" But humor was lost on Linus.

"That'll come out of your pay," he grumbled, as he snatched a wad of napkins from the counter. "Go serve the table with the three kids over there."

I inhaled, shot Lucy a forced smile, and stepped over to the table where three moms with toddlers were having morning coffee. I took their orders, catching a small glass of orange juice before it spilled, and doing my best to put on a smile despite the fact that my head pounded from lack of sleep, my stomach growled in hunger, and I felt like bursting into tears.

I turned to go to the kitchen to place the order with Lucy following me.

"I didn't get to tell you who that was," she hissed in my ear. "It was —"

"Annabelle!" boomed a familiar voice.

Oh, for God's sake.

I closed my eyes, stifling another groan, as Lucy grabbed my hand and squeezed.

Her high-pitched voice piped up. "She's working, Gavin. Bug off!"

I bit the side of my cheek to keep from smiling. I adored Lucy.

Gavin, true to form, ignored her as he plunked down on one of the spindly chairs by the bar. "Cup of coffee, baby," he said. "You know how I like my breakfast." Gavin Montgomery, the local news reporter and small town heartbreaker, flicked his fingers across his cell phone, tipping his head to the side with a cocky grin. He tapped the phone, and a flash illuminated his straight white teeth. As always, he was dressed impeccably, in a tailor-made suit, blue button-down shirt and tie, his hair perfectly coiffed. He was like a small-town Superman in designer duds.

"Selfie of the day, Gavin?" I muttered. "And no, I don't know what your usual is."

Sliding his phone in his pocket, he smoothed out the nonexistent wrinkles from his suit. "Egg white omelette, lean ham, and fruit bowl, baby."

"Linus doesn't carry lean ham, Gavin," I said. "You know what he carries. Standard breakfast sausage and bacon. And I'm not your baby."

Gavin frowned. "All those nitrates. Is he at least carrying free-range eggs yet? Or still in the dark ages?"

"Dark ages."

He shook his head and reached for my hand. His fingers were cold, his palm clammy, and I yanked my hand out of his.

"I'm working, Gavin," I chided. "Let me put in your or—"

But he was too fast. His hand snaked to my waist and pulled me to his side. "I know you're working, baby," he drawled. "But why don't you meet me for dinner tonight? I'll take you to a new little sushi restaurant over the bridge in town. We can drown our woes in sake and get to know one another a bit more."

"I don't like fish, and I despise sake," I lied. Though it was true I hated fish, I'd never tried sake in my life.

He frowned, his pretty blue eyes looking hurt. Damn him. "How could you not like fish?" he said, with a shrug. " It'll help you keep your girlish figure even after you bear children, you know."

My jaw dropped open. "Bear children? I'm only twenty years old, Gavin!"

He shrugged a shoulder, scoffing. "That's perfect. The younger you are when you bear them, the quicker you'll snap back into shape. Why not give it a whirl?"

I pulled away from him. "Putting in your order," I said, ignoring him as he continued to extrapolate on the benefits of women of childbearing years eating fish.

Lucy sidled up to me. "Can I spill his coffee on him?" The reminder of my early morning accident had me groaning out loud.

"God, don't remind me," I moaned.

"Remind you of what?" she asked, but just at then two things happened at once. My phone buzzed in my pocket at the very moment I heard a horrible screeching sound outside the diner, followed by shattering glass, wrenching metal, and shouts coming from outside. I pulled my phone out of my pocket. A text from my sister.

Mom is missing.

A feeling of dread pooling in the pit of my stomach, I tossed my notebook in my apron pocket, and ignoring shouts from Linus and pleas from Gavin, I ran outside with Lucy to see what had happened

My heart stuttered in my chest.

Just around the bend where I'd run into the huge jerk this

morning were two cars twisted sickeningly, and one of them I knew all too well: my mom's old navy Buick, the one I'd carefully hidden the keys for the night before. The other? The most expensive-looking car I'd ever laid eyes on.

I raced to the scene of the accident as sirens screamed in the background and onlookers crowded around the cars.

"Mom!" Was she okay? God! She wasn't supposed to drive. She couldn't be trusted not to hurt herself, or anyone else. The dash was demolished, and windshield shattered. Oh, God. If she hurt herself...if she hurt anyone else...

"Annabelle!" My mom's wobbly voice came from the left, and when I turned, my eyes widened in disbelief. No way. No how.

God, *NO.*

My mom stood next to the man whose coffee I'd spilled this morning, his white shirt still drenched with the dark brown liquid. My mother rushed toward me, as his eyes narrowed on mine, his enormous arms crossing his chest.

"Mom, are you okay?" I asked, looking over her frail body. She was still wearing her pale blue pajamas, and a pair of slippers, her gray-streaked hair tied back in a messy ponytail, no glasses in sight. *God.* Where was Melody?

"I'm fine," my mom said, with a wave of her hand. "But *this* one over here thinks it's fine to run stop lights. He ought to be put in jail!" She glared at the man, whose eyes narrowed even further. His jaw clenched as he glared right back at her, pulling his phone out of his pocket and putting it up to his ear. He pointed one angry finger at me, commanding me to stay right where I was.

There was no need. I wasn't going anywhere.

As police cars pulled up with flashing blue and red lights, I grimaced, and a stranger stepped up to me, an elderly woman with a raincoat pulled tight about her. "She's at fault, ma'am," she said. "I saw the whole thing."

"You hush your mouth!" my mom began.

I put a placating hand on her arm. In the early stages of dementia, my mom was in no position to be driving, let alone giving an accurate account of what happened, which was why I'd hidden the keys to begin with. My sister was supposed to be on duty.

"Mom, please be quiet," I whispered, trying my best to keep my cool, when the big beast of a man shut off his phone and stalked over to us, joined by two police officers and a paramedic crew.

His deep voice commanded the situation, as all eyes went to him. "The light turned green, and I began to drive," he said, "when this ancient piece of junk slammed right into my passenger side."

"How dare you call me an ancient piece –"

He held up a hand. "I'm talking about your *car,* not you. Please do not interrupt me. Fortunately, I was alone and it appears no one was truly hurt. The cars, on the other hand, are totaled." His eyes narrowed on me. "Am I to presume that you are the one responsible for this woman?" His gaze wandered over her pajamas and slippers.

I swallowed, embarrassed by my mother's display, horrified at the damage she'd caused, but furious at his dismissal of the one person I loved more than anyone in the entire world.

"Yes," I said, through clenched teeth. "This is my *mother.*" I glared back at him, defying him to insult my own flesh and blood. His eyes narrowed on me, but he said nothing.

"Annabelle," Officer Jones said gently. I went to school with this guy, and knew him well. With a sigh, I looked at him and nodded. "We've talked about this before, okay? Allowing your mother to drive like this, without supervision, is very dangerous."

"Matthew," I began. "I—" but it was too late. My mother heard all.

"How dare you talk about me as if I'm a child?" she said, her voice carrying over the crowd as my hand goes to her arm, attempting to calm her.

"Mom—"

"I am no older than your mother, Officer, and I am perfectly capable of driving. If *this* one over here hadn't been driving like such an idiot, we wouldn't have gotten into an accident!"

I sighed with practiced patience. "Mom, calm down. We need to get you examined," I said, hoping to distract her. I looked to Matthew. "Can we give a report at the hospital?" I asked him.

He nodded. "Of course, Annabelle. I think they both should be checked out. Mrs. Symphony, try to relax, and we'll bring you in to make sure you're okay." He turned to the big guy who was still glowering as if he were ready to breathe fire. "And you, let's get you looked over as well."

I turned my back to both of them, closing my eyes as the paramedics looked over Mom.

His car was worth more than my entire house. How would we ever get out of this?

Read more here: Beauty's Daddy: A Beauty and the Beast Adult Fairy Tale

ABOUT THE AUTHOR

USA Today bestselling author Jane Henry pens stern but loving alpha heroes, feisty heroines, and emotion-driven happily-ever-afters. She writes what she loves to read: kink with a tender touch. Jane is a hopeless romantic who lives on the East Coast with a houseful of children and her very own Prince Charming.

Sign up for Jane's newsletter, and get a free read! Sign up *HERE*.

Have you joined my Facebook reader group? We have exclusive giveaways, cover reveals, Advanced Reader Copies, and visits from your favorite authors. Come on over Join the Club!

Bookbub

Website

Amazon author page

Goodreads

Facebook

Instagram

Twitter

OTHER TITLES BY JANE YOU MAY ENJOY:

Contemporary fiction

The Billionaire Daddies Trilogy

Beauty's Daddy: A Beauty and the Beast Adult Fairy Tale

Mafia Daddy: A Cinderella Adult Fairy Tale

Dungeon Daddy: A Rapunzel Adult Fairy Tale

The Boston Doms

My Dom (Boston Doms Book 1)

His Submissive (Boston Doms Book 2)

Her Protector (Boston Doms Book 3)

His Babygirl (Boston Doms Book 4)

His Lady (Boston Doms Book 5)

Her Hero (Boston Doms Book 6)

My Redemption (Boston Doms Book 7)

Begin Again (Bound to You Book 1)

Come Back to Me (Bound to You Book 2)

Complete Me (Bound To You Book 3)

Bound to You (Boxed Set)

Black Light: Roulette Redux

Sunstrokes: Four Hot Tales of Punishment and Pleasure (Anthology)

A Thousand Yesses

Westerns

Her Outlaw Daddy

Claimed on the Frontier

Surrendered on the Frontier

Cowboy Daddies: Two Western Romances

Science Fiction

Aldric: A Sci-Fi Warrior Romance (Heroes of Avalere Book 1)

Idan: A Sci-Fi Warrior Romance (Heroes of Avalere Book 2)